PU

Migh

Clare Bevan was born ... re she still lives with her husband, son Ben, and cats. Previously a teacher, Clare has an Open University degree. Her main hobby is amateur dramatics, and she has written many plays, sketches and monologues. *Mightier than the Sword*, won the Kathleen Fidler Award and was the first book Clare wrote.

Other books by Clare Bevan

ASK ME NO QUESTIONS
JUST LIKE SUPERMAN

MIGHTIER
than the
SWORD

Clare Bevan

PUFFIN BOOKS

'The pen is mightier than the sword.'

For Martin,
who is my own knight in shining armour

PUFFIN BOOKS

Published by the Penguin Group
Penguin Books Ltd, 27 Wrights Lane, London W8 5TZ, England
Penguin Books USA Inc., 375 Hudson Street, New York, New York 10014, USA
Penguin Books Australia Ltd, Ringwood, Victoria, Australia
Penguin Books Canada Ltd, 10 Alcorn Avenue, Toronto, Ontario, Canada M4V 3B2
Penguin Books (NZ) Ltd, 182–190 Wairau Road, Auckland 10, New Zealand

Penguin Books Ltd, Registered Offices: Harmondsworth, Middlesex, England

First published by Blackie and Son Ltd 1989
Published in Puffin Books 1991
10 9 8

Text copyright © Clare Bevan, 1989
All rights reserved

Printed in England by Clays Ltd, St Ives plc

Contents

1   Pendragon

In a way, I suppose you could say that the cat started it. Although, come to think of it, I never would have called her Pendragon if it hadn't been for Mr Milner's story sessions, so perhaps he was really the one to blame after all.

In any case, I'm only writing this to show you I wasn't crazy that autumn, whatever anyone else might say. If strange things happened, then that certainly wasn't my fault. So if you think you can find a better way to explain all the coincidences that came about, then you can go right ahead. But I know what I think.

Anyway, as I say, it all began with the cat. Not that she looked like a cat when we first opened the door, because all we saw was an old cardboard box. It had been dumped on the doorstep and it was wobbling slightly. Mum immediately groaned. 'Oh no,' she said. 'Not again.'

People are always leaving things on our doorstep, you see. Their unwanted problems mostly. All the old junk they can't get rid of in any other way. Dustbin bags full of winter coats and smelling of mothballs. Bundles of faded curtains, rolls of stair carpet, whole armies of wellington boots.

Once, someone left an entire sideboard, complete

with its bowl of plastic fruit. The wooden monstrosity stood half on the path and half on the step, with a note taped to one of its drawers: 'Thought you would like this for the church roof.' My mum nearly had a fit that time, but Dad kept perfectly calm as usual.

'Never mind, love,' he said, patting her arm and then patting the sideboard as if it had feelings too. 'You know how it is. People like to think their family treasures are going to a good home. That's why they bring them to the rectory. They know we'll be grateful. And after all, this could make us a fortune at the next jumble sale.'

It didn't. It ended up on the village bonfire, and my mum made sure she lit the first flame. 'At least we sold the fruit bowl,' Dad kept reminding her, 'so it wasn't a complete failure.'

Pendragon was a much trickier problem. For one thing, she was even uglier than the sideboard. And for another, she made it clear that she had come to stay for good. She smelt of musty pilchards, she purred like a blocked drain, and she fell in love with my father as soon as he opened the box. 'It's my dog-collar that does it,' he told us. 'Makes me irresistible to females.'

Certainly, Pendragon couldn't get enough of him. She used to wrap herself round his neck like a frayed scarf and sing down his ears while he wrote his sermons. In the end, Mum almost fell for Pendragon's charms herself, and would leave tasty snacks round the house in chipped saucers.

I often wondered who could have abandoned such a loving pet, but the message scribbled on the side of her box didn't give us any real clues. 'Please take care of me. My owner can't afford to look after me any more,' was all it said. She brought with her one chewed towel, one small tin of evaporated milk, and one battered catnip mouse.

When we realized we were stuck with her, we began to argue over names. 'Jezebel, or Rebecca, or Tabitha,' Dad suggested. He always chose names out of the Bible. We once had a canary called Moses, and a pair of gerbils called Cain and Abel.

'No,' said Mum. 'Let's think of something suitable for an orphan. Annie, or Jane Eyre, or . . .'

'Come off it.' That was Kit, my older brother, interrupting. His real name is Christian Isaac Tompkins, so you can see why we called him Kit. 'That cat is definitely a witch's familiar. Look at the way she casts spells over Dad. I reckon we should call her something a bit sinister. Hecate, or Lady Macbeth, or Mother Shipton.'

That was when I chipped in. 'Mr Milner's been reading us *The Tales Of The Round Table*,' I said. 'And Arthur was an orphan too. Merlin the magician left him on the doorstep of Sir Ector's castle.'

Kit sniffed sarcastically. 'What, in a cardboard box?'

'No, of course not,' I said. 'Anyway, that's not the point. According to the book, Arthur was really the son of Uther Pendragon, the King of England. Only no one knew that until he grew up.'

This time, Kit laughed. 'Well, we can't call her Arthur, can we?' he said. 'She's confused enough as it is. She already thinks she's a neck warmer.'

'Let's call her Pendragon, then,' I said.

Mum stood up, looking pleased. 'I like that. It's a

bit unusual,' she said. So we opened a tin of sardines by way of a christening party, and Pendragon ate the lot. Which either meant that she liked her new name, or that she knew when she was on to a good thing.

And that's how everything began. Because it was around this time I was trying to impress Mr Milner with a decent piece of homework. It was only the usual, boring sort of weekend assignment, but I felt like giving him a surprise. It was his last term at our school before he retired, you see, and even though we all played him up now and then, we liked him a lot.

He was a really old-fashioned teacher, but in a nice way. Nervous of computers and all the new electrical gadgets around the school, but very quiet and patient with us. And full of interesting stories.

Until I went up into his class, I was always dead untidy. My books looked as though someone had run over them with a steam roller, and my writing was splattered over the pages like spray-on graffiti. Of course, that was mainly because I'd never taken much trouble to make it any different, but I have got some excuses.

For a start, I can't help being a bit clumsy. I was born with this thing called spina bifida, which means I can't walk too well, and I spend most of my time in a wheelchair. I can heave myself around on a walking frame, but I'm not too keen on using that, so I'm always getting into trouble for not taking enough exercise. Which is true, if you're only thinking about my legs. But my arms get plenty of work when they're pushing my wheels along, and even Kit has to admit he's jealous of my muscles these days.

The problem is, once your hands get used to shoving

a loaded wheelchair about, they tend to use a pen like a pneumatic drill, and that isn't good news if you want to win any prizes for neatness. All my other teachers had nagged me for hours, or else given up and let me use a typewriter instead. But Mr Milner never could trust machines, so he kept looking for other ways around the difficulty: special carpentry pencils, or pens with rubber bands round them. Things like that. And he put a ban on ballpoints altogether.

'Dreadful inventions,' he called them. 'Abominations. But I think I might just have the solution tucked away in a drawer at home somewhere.'

Well, after all that, I felt I ought to make some sort of an effort too. So on the evening of the christening, I left Pendragon to breathe her fishy fumes over the rest of the family, and trundled off to my own room for a bit of peace.

One of the best things about being a rector's son is that we always live in enormous houses with wide hallways and loads of rooms. This isn't because we're rich. We don't own the houses. We just stay in them for a few years, until my father moves on to his next church. But it means I've generally got plenty of space for my wheelchair, and a downstairs room to myself. In this particular house, it was really a study, overlooking the garden, and it was supposed to be the Sermon Room. But Dad said he preferred to do his writing upstairs in the attic, so he didn't mind the swap.

I had my bed by the window and my portable TV wedged in the fireplace, but there wasn't much else. Someone had built a gigantic wooden desk all along

11

one wall, and that took up most of the rest of the space. It had all sorts of little shelves and compartments, which I suppose were meant to hold spare Bibles and bottles of ink, but I filled them with football cards and cassettes and stuff like that.

I was fond of that desk, because the writing surface was at exactly the right height for my elbows, and the wood had a warm, friendly smell to it. Under the thick layers of waxy polish, I could see hundreds of dents where other people had pressed their pens into paper, years before. It was impossible to feel lonely sitting there. In fact, I almost enjoyed doing my homework, so long as it wasn't anything too brain-straining.

This time, it was dead easy. Or should have been. All we had to do was write a short story and give it an illustration at the end. There were three titles to choose from, all of them completely useless. Mr Milner must have been setting the same headings for the last fifty years: 'My Pets', 'The Best Day Of The Holiday', and 'A Hero From History'.

I opened my book, accidentally buckled the corner of the page with my sleeve, and chewed the end of my pen. My head had gone a total blank. Our only pet was probably dozing on the boiler by now, and dreaming about tinned fish. Hardly an inspiring subject. And the best day of our holiday had been the day we drove home, after a week of pouring rain. I had been doing my best to forget that.

So I was left with the third option. Unfortunately, the only historical characters I knew were Julius Caesar and Henry VIII, but I didn't think I could call either of them heroes. I mean, one got stabbed to death by his best friends, and the other spent his time eating chicken legs and executing his wives.

I took my pen apart to waste a minute or two, lost the little spring that held it together, and decided to use a pencil instead. The only one I could find needed sharpening, so that helped to pass a bit more time, and by then I was beginning to get fidgety. There was a good series on the TV in half an hour, and if I didn't get a move on, I knew I wouldn't finish the work at all. Not that I was scared of Mr Milner. No one was. But I couldn't bear it when his face went all crumpled and disappointed.

'Well, well, Adam. I am surprised at you. Very surprised indeed,' he would say.

Comments like that tended to make my face go purple, and I never knew where to look. So I made up my mind to write something, even if it turned out to be rubbish. Then I thought of Pendragon again, and the Camelot stories. That was it. I realized that King Arthur wasn't a proper historical character, more of a legend, but everyone knows that legends are supposed to be based on truth so I didn't think I was stretching the point too far.

I smoothed out the page as much as I could and wrote my title. 'The True Born King.' The first couple of sentences were just routine stuff. 'My favourite historical hero is King Arthur because . . .' You know the sort of thing. But after that I started to get really involved, and my hand had to move faster and faster to keep up with the ideas tumbling out of my mind. Ideas that must have been hiding away inside my head somewhere for years, waiting for a chance to escape.

'When he was young, he was bossed about by his older brother, Sir Kay, and he always felt a misfit although he didn't know why. His father, Sir Ector, was kind to him, but all the time Arthur knew he was the odd one out. One day, at a great tournament, his brother sent him to fetch a weapon, but Arthur pulled a magic sword out of a stone. This proved he was the true born king of all England, and Merlin appeared to tell everyone who Arthur really was. The son of King Uther Pendragon.'

Now I came to the important part. The part that made the roots of my hair tingle.

'So King Arthur is my hero because I feel just like him. My big brother bosses me about, and he does all the things I can't do, like jogging and football and cycling. So sometimes I think I might have been left on the doorstep of the rectory for my family to find. Arthur was adopted by Sir Ector, and I was adopted by a rector, and that's nearly the same thing, isn't it? But one day I'm going to surprise everyone, just like Arthur did, and then I'll find out who I really am.'

At that point I stopped, because the alarm on my watch was pinging, and it was time for my TV programme. Only, now I wasn't in a hurry to turn it on. Instead, I sat where I was, staring at my story and thinking over what I had written. It was all true. I had always felt a misfit. The odd one out. Not just because of my wheelchair, although that was part of it. But there were other reasons too. My hair for one thing. Anyone can see it's the wrong colour. Mum and Dad are both dark, like Kit, but I'm a sort of pale mousy brown and my skin's all white and freckly, especially in the summer. I never go tanned and healthy-looking like everyone else. Just red and blotchy with bits of flaky skin on my nose.

The room was beginning to grow gloomy now, and when I spun my chair I could see a faint picture of myself reflected in the windows. There was no doubt about it. I was definitely different from all the rest of my family. An orphan, abandoned by someone desperate for help who had sworn my parents to secrecy.

I pulled the curtains behind me, so that I was folded in a dark cave facing the night garden. My heart was thumping away in my chest and my stomach was doing high dives. Perhaps I was the child of someone famous: an escaped criminal, on the run, and cruelly convicted for a crime he had never committed; a foreign princess, forced to hide me from her enemies despite her love for me; a poverty-stricken couple who had fled to another country to seek their fortune, and who were at this very moment discovering a priceless goldmine. Soon, they would return to claim me, and I would become the richest boy in the whole of Europe.

I liked that idea. Kit would have to come to me begging for pocket money, and I would buy the family a house of their own in gratitude for all their kindness. It was such a satisfying daydream that I was half-way to believing it when something tickled the back of my neck and made me gasp with shock.

I reversed myself into the room again and realized the intruder was only Pendragon. She had climbed up the back of my chair and was trying to eat the collar of my sweater. 'Gerroff, you daft thing,' I grumbled. She smelt more fishy than ever, but before I could push her off she started to purr, and I came over all sentimental.

'You and me,' I whispered as she settled herself

round my neck. 'We're in this together, Pendragon. Two of a kind.' And we shared a packet of sausage-flavoured crisps while we watched the second half of my programme.

I felt quite peculiar at breakfast next morning. Almost like a visitor in a strange hotel. I kept noticing more and more things about my family that made them different from me. Take Kit, for instance. He was slurping his way through a horrible great bowl of porridge. Porridge. I can't stand the stuff. It looks like a bubbling swamp in a horror movie, and it tastes even worse. I never touch it. I've seen what it can do to the inside of a saucepan, and how anybody can swallow something like that is a total mystery to me.

So as far as I was concerned, that proved I couldn't be Kit's real brother. I was much too sensible. And then there was Dad. He was just fiddling around with a slice of cold toast, and drinking about a gallon of black coffee. Revolting. And Mum was almost as bad. With her, it was a bowl of tasteless muesli, soaked overnight until it had gone all sludgy and disgusting. What a thing to eat, when you're supposed to be setting other people a good example.

In fact, I was the only normal person in the house that day. I had a boiled egg and cornflakes, tea and hot toast. See what I mean? Usually I would have taken ages munching my way through it all, while everyone else charged round the kitchen. But just for once I was in a hurry. I couldn't wait to get to school and tell my friends what I had discovered.

As it turned out, they took a bit of convincing.

Jenny Morgan was the first. She thumped me in the arm and told me I was cracked.

'Don't be so daft,' she said. 'Of course you're not adopted. Everybody has that idea sometime. When I was little, I thought I was really the daughter of a beautiful pop star, who'd lost me at a concert and sworn never to sing again until she found me. But I knew it was only a dream. I grew out of that sort of thing years ago. Along with the Tooth Fairy and Father Christmas.'

I suppose that was meant to make me shrivel up and feel small, but it didn't work. 'Just because you were wrong, doesn't mean to say I'm wrong too,' I argued. 'One day I'm going to surprise everyone. I'll be exactly like King Arthur, and then you'll be sorry you didn't believe me.'

'How can you be like King Arthur?' asked Lanky Lockhead, arriving late and missing the point as usual. 'Your name's Adam. I've never heard of a king called Adam before.'

But I wasn't going to be squashed all that easily. 'Adam Richard Tompkins, actually,' I said. 'A. R. T. See? And that's short for Arthur, isn't it?'

Lanky's face went through about fifteen changes, while he juggled with the idea. Confusion, realization, doubt, then confusion again. Spelling never was his strong point. 'What're we talking about anyway?' he said in the end.

I started to explain, but puzzles are always a headache for Lanky, and he was still looking baffled when Mr Milner rang the bell for morning lessons.

At break, we began the conversation again, from where we had left it. 'Oh, I think I get you now,' said

Lanky in triumph. 'You think you're like Oliver Twist in the workhouse, only you're really a millionaire in disguise.'

'Well, something like that,' I agreed. 'But Mum and Dad aren't cruel to me or anything. I just don't think they're my real parents, that's all.'

Lanky nibbled thoughtfully through a handful of salted peanuts while he worked that one out. He's very tall and gangly, with a blob of fair hair on top of his head, and he does everything in slow motion. When he walks, he looks like a worried stick insect balancing on a twig. He swallowed the last peanut, licked the ends of his fingers and finally gave his opinion. 'You're mad.'

'Oh, thanks very much,' I said. 'With friends like you, who needs enemies?'

Lanky made the croaky, groaning noise he uses for a laugh. 'Well,' he said, 'what do you expect? I used to think I was the long-lost son of a master spy, till someone told my dad. He reckoned it was the best joke he'd ever heard. He reckoned he'd been trying to lose me for years, but no one would take me away. That's what he reckoned.'

'OK, OK,' I said. I was getting pretty fed up by this time. If even people like Lanky had once had daydreams about doorsteps, then perhaps I really was being stupid.

'That's right. You tell him, Lanky,' said Jenny, who happened to be passing. She's only small, but she's got the biggest ears in the universe, and they're always flapping. 'He's crazy if you ask me.'

'Well, I didn't ask you, if you must know,' I said.

'You wait. I'll prove I'm telling the truth and then you'll have to listen.'

That was a mistake. Jenny was never one to miss a challenge. The next minute, she was sprinting across the field to round up the rest of our gang. 'Oi, you lot,' she was calling. 'Come and have a laugh. Adam wants to prove he's King Arthur in disguise.'

Of course, I tried to complain. 'Trust you to exaggerate,' I shouted. 'All I said was. . . .' But it was already too late. And in any case, it didn't matter, because the laugh was on her. All the others came stampeding over to us, looking really excited.

'Great idea, Adam,' said Gary One, slapping me on the back. 'We'll be the knights. What shall we use for a Round Table?'

'Let's go and have a tournament with Miss Lane's class,' said Gary Two. 'We could flatten them, easy.'

'Yeah,' said Gary Three. 'I'll be the Champion and chop everyone's heads off for you.'

There were three Garys in our class that year, and they had been particularly bored all morning. This was because Gary Three had kicked Gary One's football on to the school roof, and it was going to take about six years before Old Miseryguts, the caretaker, got round to knocking it down again. So any idea, however loony, was bound to brighten things up.

'We could meet after school,' I suggested. 'Down by the village pond. We can use that for the enchanted lake.'

'And the picnic benches under the big tree can be the table,' added Tracey Fletcher, who had just joined us. She was one of Jenny's best friends, and also the

19

biggest person in the class, so it was usually wise to agree with her.

'Yeah,' said Gary Three. So that was settled.

Once we got back to the classroom, the three Garys launched into a sword fight with their rulers, and Lanky went to practise dramatic death scenes in the quiet corner. I was being wheeled round the room by a boy called Perry, who could do brilliant trumpet impersonations, and Jenny was sitting on the radiator pretending to ignore us. I could tell she was in an awkward mood by the way she was nibbling the ends of her hair. Still, that was her problem. We were having fun.

When Mr Milner came in, he gave us one of his surprised-and-disappointed looks, so we all calmed down and waited for him to polish the seat of his chair with the class duster. For some reason, he always did that before he began a lesson. Perhaps he had once sat on a custard pie, and had been checking for booby traps ever since.

As soon as he was ready, he asked us to gather round his desk, so I parked my chair in the front row, and everyone else pushed and shoved to get a decent view. He was holding up a peculiar sort of pen. It was made from a dull, mottled metal which seemed to change colour whenever it caught the light, and its barrel was squat and stumpy between Mr Milner's thin fingers.

But the nib was the oddest part. Broad and blunt, with a central split to carry the ink to the paper.

'Who would like to try it?' Mr Milner's eyes were all crinkled up, and I had a feeling this could be some kind of trick. An exploding pen, maybe, that would fire ink up your nose as soon as you pressed on it. Or a programmed nib that would only write backwards. I kept quiet and waited for someone else to volunteer.

I didn't have to wait for long. Three of Jenny's friends were already waving their hands in the air and saying, 'Oooh, ooh,' in squeaky voices. Mr Milner smiled, and handed them the pen without a word. They all looked extremely smug and confident, which wasn't surprising because they all had incredibly neat writing. Their topic books were good enough to frame and hang on the wall, whereas mine was only fit for the school incinerator.

There was a pile of spare paper on Mr Milner's desk, so each of the girls took a turn at writing a short message. 'My name is Tracey.' Enthralling stuff like that. You should have seen their faces. One by one, the smug grins faded as they passed the pen to a fresh victim. The paper was covered in blobs and blots and thick, crawly squiggles, as though a spider full of black blood had just been horribly murdered.

'Jennifer Morgan?' Mr Milner offered the pen to Jenny, but she wouldn't touch it. She didn't want to look a fool.

'Gary?' All three boys shook their heads and backed away. Only Lanky was daft enough to step forwards. He wasn't really volunteering, just stepping into the gap, but he didn't get a chance to protest.

'Lance Lockhead', he wrote on a clean page. At least, I suppose that was what he wrote, but no one could have said for sure. Mr Milner gave him the duster to mop the ink off his fingers.

'Anyone else?'

Silence. I sat very still and tried to read the register

upside down. But my neck soon began to tingle, and I knew it wouldn't matter how much I sank into my chair or thought distant thoughts. I was doomed. I could feel Mr Milner's eyes boring holes into the top of my head, and when I looked up he was all ready to pounce.

He stretched out the pen towards me and slid the paper under my nose. 'Your turn, Art.' His voice was very soft and secretive. For a moment I was so stunned I couldn't refuse. Art! That was what he had said. No one had ever called me by that name before, and yet it felt absolutely right and comfortable. Could he have overheard me in the playground that morning? If so, he wasn't half as deaf as he sometimes pretended.

I took the pen from him and settled it in my left hand. It was warm from use, and pleasantly rounded. I slotted it behind my thumb and pulled myself closer towards the desk. Everyone was watching me, but I wasn't particularly bothered. After all, my effort couldn't be much worse than Lanky's.

I was trying to remember all the tips Mr Milner had taught me over the last few weeks. Relax. Set the page at an angle so you can see what you're doing. Don't grip too hard. Press as you make the downward stroke, then let the nib slide smoothly upwards again. I leaned over and wrote, 'The True Born King.' Then I sat back to inspect the results. Not bad. Not bad at all.

Suddenly, I realized that the buzzing noises I could hear weren't inside my own head, but were coming from the rest of the class.

'Good old Art,' said Lanky, giving me a nudge. He sounded quite proud. The girls were staring at me as though I had just arrived from another planet, and the Garys were beginning to snigger.

'How did you manage that?' asked Jenny in amazement. 'Usually, you can't write for toffee. You must have cheated.'

'How could I?' I said. 'I just picked it up and wrote with it, the same as everyone else.' Mind you, I was feeling quite puzzled myself.

'Quiet.' Mr Milner held up his hand for silence, and when most of the fuss had died down he said, 'This is a rather special pen. Quite old and somewhat unusual. It's not like your modern pens. Nasty, mass-produced rubbish. This was made by craftsmen, and designed for left-handed people. It's been in my family for many years, but I've never used it myself because I'm right-handed.'

He gave me one of those quick smiles that friends use, then he added, 'I've been waiting to find a good home for it. Perhaps you would like to keep it, Art? It seems to have chosen you all by itself.'

I could feel my face going pink, and I just sat gaping at him for a second or two. I mean, I'm not the sort of person who wins prizes. Not even in the church bazaar. I've never gone home with so much as a tin of baked beans before, and now I was being awarded an antique pen.

It was still lodged under my thumb, so I lifted it up and held it in my palms. It seemed really valuable to me. The clip had been made in the shape of a tiny sword, and the nib looked as if it might be genuine gold.

'Thanks, Mr Milner,' I managed to gasp at last. 'It's brilliant. I'll take good care of it for you. Honest.'

'Of course you will,' he said. 'Because it's yours now.'

The room had become very still. Almost solemn. It was as if something wonderfully important had happened, instead of just a silly handwriting competition. But then Mr Milner broke the spell.

'Come on, you horrible lot,' he announced in his normal crackly voice. 'To work. Story books out, and let's hear some of that homework you were going to write for me.'

The others went scrambling back to their places, but I hung about for the mob to clear before I span my chair round. I was preparing to move when Mr Milner took the handles and steered me back to my own desk. As he did so, he leaned his head close to my ear. 'Use it well, lad,' he whispered. 'Use it well.'

I nodded, and held the pen even more tightly. I didn't want to drop it under my wheels or anything like that, and now that my hands were free, I took my first really close look at it. The casing smelt metallic and inky, and as I ran my thumbnail over its surface, I could detect a row of small indentations. A word had been engraved into the barrel. Once, the letters had probably been painted in gold or silver, but any colours had long since been worn away.

When Mr Milner parked my chair, I raised the pen to catch the light from the classroom window, and it was then I first read the name.

Now, it's up to you whether you want to believe this, but you can always check with Jenny if you think I'm making it up. But I promise you, there it was as clear as day. A line of tiny, dark dents. And the word they made was 'Excalibur'.

2 The Round Table

I didn't offer to read out my story. It was too personal, and in any case I was beginning to feel a bit queasy about it. Only last night I had been imagining myself as a modern King Arthur, and now here I was with Excalibur in my hands. So you can see what I mean by coincidences, and that was only the first.

Anyway, I spent the lesson copying out my homework with the new pen, and drawing pictures of swords and shields all round the border. The finished result was quite effective, even if I say so myself. That pen seemed to have a will of its own, and everything I wrote with it came out looking old-fashioned and fancy. I think it must have been something to do with the wide nib, which could make lines of any thickness, depending on how you held it.

I was feeling pretty pleased with myself by the time the bell went for lunch, and I could tell Mr Milner was impressed too. He didn't actually say much, but he kept nodding and making funny noises in the back of his throat, which was just as good. I roared off down the corridor with my elbows steaming, and met the rest of the gang outside.

'Let's have a look at your pen,' said Lanky. 'I reckon it's really weird.'

I took Excalibur out of my top pocket and handed it over, while the others crowded round to make rude comments. That's what friends are for.

'It's weird all right,' said Gary One. 'It's got a nib like a screwdriver.'

'Like a shovel,' said Gary Two.

'Yeah,' said Gary Three. 'You'd better not leave it lying around, or someone'll nick it to dig up the road.'

Jenny was the only one who didn't say anything, and I had a feeling she might be a bit jealous. But then Old Miseryguts came across with a dustbin-bag full of mouldy tennis balls and odd plimsolls he'd collected off the roof, so that put everyone in a better mood. They went charging away for a quick game of football before the dinner whistle, while I did a couple of laps round the edge of the field. I was feeling energetic for once.

Inside my head, I was galloping through the countryside on a pure white charger, slaying dragons and rescuing maidens in distress. Unfortunately, the only maidens within reach were Jenny and her crowd, but they were too busy beating the boys at football to need rescuing from anyone. I wasn't bothered. I could wait. And so could my four-wheeled horse.

But there wasn't any more talk of swords and knights and round tables until the very end of the afternoon, when Mr Milner adjusted his half-moon glasses and went to sit on the radiator. That was the signal for his story session, so we shoved our work away in our boxes, wriggled around in our seats to get comfortable, and generally tried to look interested.

We weren't doing this because we were naturally well-behaved or polite. Far from it. Most of us were experts at driving our teachers round the bend, and every one of us had perfected an irritating little habit or three. But we hardly ever used these tricks on Mr Milner, particularly when he was reading to us. He had a way of telling stories that made them come alive. Not because he waved his arms around or tried to act out all the characters. In fact, he usually sat absolutely still, and spoke in such a soft voice you felt you were the only other person in the room.

Sometimes, when he looked in my direction, I could sense shivers in the top part of my spine where the nerves still work properly. And the room would fill with ghosts or monsters, or whatever else he happened to be describing. I think he must have known most of those stories off by heart, because he hardly ever bothered to glance at the book, although he turned the pages as he went along.

I don't know anyone who didn't enjoy those sessions. That afternoon, he was telling us what happened to Arthur after he had pulled the sword out of the stone. Apparently, his bossy brother Sir Kay started to tell everyone that he'd won the sword himself, but when they made him put it back in the stone it got stuck again, and only Arthur could budge it. So that settled the argument, and although everyone moaned about having such a young king, Merlin insisted on a coronation.

Then Arthur promised to go round righting wrongs and driving out evil from the land, so Merlin gave him three gifts. To be the best of knights, to be the greatest of kings, and to live longer than anyone else in the world.

That was all pretty straightforward, but then the

complications started. The very first time he tried to do a good deed, Arthur had his sword smashed up by a mad knight called Sir Pellinore. Merlin sent the knight off in search of a Questing Beast, and took Arthur down to the shores of an enchanted lake. Suddenly an arm dressed in white samite came popping out of the water, and waved a new sword in the air. This was Excalibur, of course, and most of us had heard that part of the story before. After all, it's pretty famous.

Well, Arthur rowed off in a magic boat to collect the sword, and when he got back, Merlin warned him that enemies would try to rob and ruin him. Arthur knew that his chief opponent was a witch called Morgana Le Fay, who was very beautiful and also very clever. But instead of worrying about it, he went straight off and got married to Queen Guinevere. Which was the boring bit of the story.

Luckily, the bell rang at that point, so we didn't have to sit through too much romantic stuff.

'When did Arthur get the Round Table then?' asked Lanky, as Mr Milner closed the book and began to polish his glasses on the end of his tie.

'You'll find out tomorrow,' was all he would say. So the rest of us groaned to please him, and started packing our bags. I put my pen in my top pocket again, so that the clip showed, and wheeled past Mr Milner's desk to say good-night. He nodded in my direction and gave me another of those quick, secretive smiles. There were hundreds of tiny folds and creases round his eyes and mouth, and at that moment he seemed to remind me of someone I had once seen in a book somewhere. Someone immensely old and wise.

'Come on, Art,' called Lanky. 'Race you to the

pond.' And mumbling something vague, I turned the chair and steamed away after my friend.

We were soon heading for the village pond, to see if it looked anything at all like the enchanted lake of Avalon. Some hopes. Normally, it looked more like a haunted swamp, with rusty bicycle wheels and stolen shopping trolleys sticking out of the slime. But that evening it seemed different. The sun was going down, and there was a thin mist hovering over the damp grass. Quite atmospheric.

And that wasn't all. On our side of the water, the horse-chestnuts were beginning to lose their leaves, but that was the only litter we could detect. Someone had scraped all the old crisp bags and sweet wrappers into a tidy heap next to the bulging litter-bin, and painted the picnic benches with fresh green paint. It all looked extremely civilised for a change.

On the other side of the water was the stretch of private land that belonged to Morgan's Folly. Jenny's two mad aunties lived there, in the peculiar round house that looked like a water tower with curtains.

'But they're not mad,' Jenny used to say. 'Just a bit cranky. And they're not my aunties. They're Great Aunties. So there.'

We reckoned they must have round carpets and round beds and round furniture all over the place, but Jenny always told us to mind our own business if we asked her any questions. I think she felt rather embarrassed about the two old ladies, and the way they dressed in wispy white clothes when they went shopping in the village stores.

'I bet they've got a proper round table,' said Lanky.

'D'you think they'd let us borrow it for one of our meetings?'

'Fat chance,' I started to say. Then I heard the rest of the gang arriving. Jenny with two of her crowd, the three Garys, a boy called Alan who collected bruises, and Perry leading the way doing his trumpet impersonations.

'Hey,' shouted Gary One, as soon as they reached us. 'Look at the conker tree. It's nearly ready.'

'Let's find some sticks,' said Gary Two, aiming a tin can into the branches.

'Yeah,' said Gary Three. 'Conkers. Just what we need for ammunition.'

'Why do we need ammunition?' asked Lanky, who had already hurt his finger on one of the spiky green shells.

'For a tournament, dumbo,' said Jenny. 'That's what knights do all day. They have mock battles so they'll be ready to fight their enemies when they go off on their adventures.'

'Oh,' said Lanky, still sucking his sore finger. 'I thought they sat round the table having banquets and telling stories all the time.'

'No,' said Perry scornfully. 'That sounds more like the seven dwarfs.'

And they all went scrabbling around in the grass collecting conkers, while I wheeled myself over to the big oak tree to look at the benches. There were several wooden seats scattered about the place, plus a circular one attached to the trunk itself. The paint still smelt wet, but it would have to do. I looked back at the others, who were busy filling their bags with prize specimens, or whizzing under-ripe missiles at one another. I could see they weren't going to be in the mood for anything organised that evening.

'Hey. You lot,' I shouted. 'Tell your mums you'll be late home tomorrow. We'll have our first Round Table meeting, and I'll give you all your new names. Then we can make some plans for a real tournament.'

'Yeah,' the three Garys shouted back, without bothering to look round.

I watched them for a few minutes longer, then shrugged and twisted my chair towards the path. There was a grassy slope in the way, and I had to push down hard against the wheels to work up any sort of speed. The ground was very soft that evening, and I was getting nowhere fast.

I tried again, and this time the chair moved surprisingly smoothly. I realized that someone must be pushing me, and guessed it was probably Lanky. 'Thanks,' I said. 'I thought I was going to be here all night.'

'No trouble.' I twisted my head, and saw that my helper was Jenny. Her face still looked serious. 'This is only a game, you know,' she said in her bossiest voice. 'All this King Arthur business. Don't get too carried away with it all, will you?'

'Don't be daft,' I said. 'I do know what I'm doing, thank you very much.' I hoped I sounded sarcastic, and I steered myself away as fast as I could to show how independent I was.

I reached the rectory before the village clock started to strike the quarter, but Kit was at the door already, looking all fit and muscular in his best track suit.

'I've just been for a run round the boundary,' he said, breathing in to make his chest seem even bigger

31

than it was already. 'You ought to take more exercise, kiddo. You'll get fat and flabby sitting around in that thing all the time.'

'Yes, yes, yes,' I grumbled. 'I get plenty of exercise if you must know. Only this lunchtime I went for a . . .' But before I could get any further, a voice interrupted me.

'Sign the petition, boys? Save our village pond from the developers.' It was the Badger Man riding up on his bike. At that time he had only just left college, and he was still trying to find a job somewhere near home. Something to do with animals, if he was lucky. He was really quite young, but for most of the time, he looked more like an old tramp. He was always burrowing around in the fields and hedges searching for free food. Part of the year he seemed to live on toadstools and dandelions, and he usually had a carrier bag full of fascinating finds. Everyone was fond of him. He knew the names of all the local plants and insects, and whenever anyone met him he always had something interesting to say.

'Good morning. The rooks are nesting low this year. Watch out for squalls.' 'Good day to you. The first blackberries are ripening nicely. Tell your mum to warm the oven.' 'Good afternoon. The hedgehogs are hibernating early. Buy yourself some thick boots.'

Today, though, he sounded worried.

'What d'you mean?' asked Kit. 'Save the village pond? It's not drying up is it?'

'It looks all right to me,' I said. 'I was down there five minutes ago and it was tidier than usual. Someone's gone and painted the seats.'

'I know,' said the Badger Man. 'It was me. But I'm afraid it's doomed all the same.'

'Doomed?' Dad had appeared now, wearing his dog collar over his gardening jumper. 'Who's doomed? Can I help?'

'Well, I hope so,' said the Badger Man. 'We can at least try.' He held up a sheet of paper, and read out the words printed along the top. 'Save our pond from the developers. Sign here if you would like to fight the plans to build an estate of holiday cottages over our local beauty spot.'

'Hm,' said Dad thoughtfully. 'I see.' Then he shook his head ruefully and added, 'It's not exactly a beauty spot though, is it? More of a public dumping ground these days.'

'I know,' admitted the Badger Man. 'The trouble is, we've all been taking it for granted. But if the whole village started to work together, I'm sure things would change for the better.' He looked so forlorn, Dad simply couldn't resist.

'All right,' he said. 'I'll sign. I suppose it's worth a try.' He began rummaging around the front of his jumper, but as he wasn't wearing his sermon jacket he had to admit defeat in the end and ask for a pen. He hated borrowing things.

'Sorry,' said Kit. His track suit was the fancy sort that doesn't have decent-sized pockets.

'Borrow mine,' I said. 'I bet you can't write with it, though.' I held out Excalibur, and Dad took it from me with a puzzled expression on his face.

'What's this?' he asked. 'Where on earth did you find it?'

'I didn't find it,' I explained proudly. 'Mr Milner gave it to me. It was a prize. For good handwriting.'

Kit practically exploded at that. 'You?' he roared. 'Good handwriting? Since when? You write like a chimpanzee in boxing gloves.'

I didn't bother to answer. I just waited while they both signed their names on the Badger Man's list. Dad was first, and he made a fair effort, but I could tell he was confused.

Then Kit tried. 'Useless,' he complained. 'This pen's duff. No wonder old Milner was throwing it out. Someone must've busted the nib.' He rammed it back in my pocket, but I took it out again.

'Can I sign too?' I asked.

'Course you can,' said the Badger Man. 'The more the merrier, that's what I say.'

So I leaned the paper on my arm-rest and wrote my full name, making the initials extra large and prominent. A. R. T. They stood out darkly against the white background and I grinned to myself.

'Well,' said Dad. 'Well, well, well, well, well.' He was obviously a bit stuck for words. And Kit wasn't much better.

He never liked to swear in front of Dad, so he was having some trouble finding a suitable way to express his feelings. In the end, the best he could manage was, 'S'truth.'

Meanwhile, I was behaving in an elaborately casual manner, as though I had always been able to write like a professional artist.

'Thanks,' said the Badger Man. By the sound of his voice, he had guessed that something unusual was happening, but he was too polite to ask questions. He scratched his head, tucked the sheet of paper in his saddle-bag, and prepared to cycle off down our path like a medieval traveller in search of adventures.

We watched him go, then I said, 'What's for tea?' I was still trying to sound relaxed and cool. But really, I was feeling quite dizzy with excitement. And more like King Arthur than ever.

Dad laughed. 'I think it's sausages,' he said. 'With home-grown spuds. And you can tell Mr Milner from me, I think he must be some sort of magician to get you to write like that. I never would have believed it. Never.' And we all went in to tea.

After the meal, I had to demonstrate my new skills to Mum, so I wrote out one of my favourite lines from the King Arthur story. 'It is called Excalibur, and none may stand against its stroke.' She liked that.

'Quite an improvement,' she said, inspecting what I had written under the kitchen light. 'I think you might turn out to be artistic after all. I wonder where you get it from. I shall have to ask your Gran.'

'Mr Milner showed me,' I said quietly, keeping my thoughts to myself. 'Anyone fancy a game of Scrabble?'

Kit groaned and flicked a soggy tea-towel at me. 'Not again,' he said. 'Why can't you play computer games like all the other kids, and leave the rest of us in peace?'

'Because I prefer word games,' I told him. 'And anyway, it's good for my spelling, isn't it, Mum?'

Kit hated playing Scrabble with me. He still does, mainly because he always loses. He'd much rather be running round a race track or working out in a gym.

He's the only person I know who asks for sets of weights for Christmas.

At that time, his bedroom looked like a torture chamber, it was so full of exercise machines, and he used to spend half his life measuring his chest. But the joke was that he still had a hard time beating me at an arm-wrestling match.

Now he was appealing to Mum for mercy. 'Look, I'm supposed to be meeting the jogging club in half an hour. I haven't got time for stupid games. Can't someone else play with him?'

'Your father's writing the Parish Magazine, and I'm making flapjacks for the Merry Ladies' Bring-and-Buy,' said Mum. 'So that just leaves you, I'm afraid. Give him one game before you leave, there's a love.'

Kit threw down his tea-towel so that it dangled limply over the boiler pipe, and I heard him muttering something hostile under his breath. 'Twenty minutes, then,' he said out loud. 'But that's the limit, right?'

'Right,' I said. 'That'll do. I should be able to beat you easy-peasy in that time.'

'And no fancy rules,' he added. 'Plurals and proper names are allowed. OK?'

'OK,' I agreed. It made no difference to me.'

Back in my room, I got the Scrabble board out and opened it on the bed. Kit sat on a bean bag and started to jumble the pieces, while I shifted Pendragon to the far end of the duvet. She grumbled a bit, made herself a new nest and began to snore almost immediately.

Of course, if Kit had used his common sense, he would have played badly on purpose, to get the game over with as quickly as possible. But once he got going, he couldn't resist putting up a fight. He's got this competitive instinct, and he never could bear to lose at any sort of game. So we ended up playing for about forty-five minutes before he remembered the time and jumped up, swearing.

'Damn, damn, damn,' he said, or words to that effect. 'Why didn't you remind me, you little pest? What's the score?'

I'd written everything down with Excalibur, but without adding it up I could see I had won. Then something clicked inside my head, and I remembered that I wasn't my ordinary self any more. I was Art, the true born king, and I could afford to be generous.

'You just managed to beat me,' I said. 'That last double letter put you two points ahead.'

'Oh,' he said, looking surprised. 'Oh, good. Well, thanks for the game then, kiddo. See you.' And he shot out of the door like a stripy bullet, in his most expensive kit. I guessed there must be a new girl at the jogging club that he wanted to impress, and I grinned to myself as I heard the front door slam.

'Good night, Sir Kay,' I thought. Then I turned back to the Scrabble board. The crossword was still laid out as we had left it, so I added up the score properly this time. I had won by a clear fifty points, and with one more go I could have used up all my remaining pieces. The word 'LOT' was already on the board, and in my hand I held a C, an M, an E and a blank.

'Camelot,' I said triumphantly, completing the word for my own satisfaction. Pendragon woke with a sigh, stretched and moved up the bed to sniff at the pieces Kit had left behind. None of them seemed much use, so I tipped everything into a heap and muddled the letters ready for the next time we played. Only, I got a bit carried away and started experimenting with different combinations.

I like anagrams, you see. Words made from other words. For instance, my mother's name is Margaret, and you can rearrange that to say stupid things like 'Mr A Great' or 'A Rat Germ.' You should try it yourself sometime. It's really good for a laugh.

I'd used all my family's names before, so this time I tried it on my friends from school. 'Lance' worked well, because it made 'Clean'. I couldn't wait to tell Lanky in the morning. Then I used 'Gary' to make 'Yarg', which is a smelly sort of cheese they sell at the village stores. I was quite pleased with that one too. But the biggest thrill came when I decided to try the trick on Mr Milner's name.

Pendragon was on my lap now, watching my every movement with her sleepy green eyes. My fingers were tingling with excitement as I set out the letters. I could see what was going to happen long before I had finished the word. In fact, I couldn't think why I had never noticed such an obvious thing weeks ago, when I first went into Mr Milner's class.

'Watch,' I whispered into the old cat's ear. And with a couple of quick changes, 'MILNER' was transformed into 'MERLIN'. Pendragon purred.

As for me, I sat gazing at the letters, and remembering what Dad had said to me when we were signing the petition.

'Tell Mr Milner I think he must be some sort of magician.'

I picked up Excalibur again, replaced the cap, and felt the sharp point of the tiny sword with the tip of my finger. 'None may stand against its stroke,' I thought. 'And with it you shall bring peace and freedom to this land.'

3   Excalibur

I didn't get too much sleep that night, I can tell you.
And when I did finally manage to nod off, it was only
to go charging into battle with a great army of knights
all dressed in silver track suits. The Badger Man came
thundering past on a bicycle shaped like a metal
horse, and he kept yelling, 'Save our pond. Drive out
evil. Right the wrongs.'

Somewhere in the distance I could hear Perry's
trumpet impersonations, and when Dad shook me
awake I was totally exhausted. I couldn't understand
where I was, or why he was hooting with laughter.
'What's so funny?' I asked him, in between the yawns.
'What's the joke?'

'Oh, nothing,' said Dad, wiping his eyes with his
thumbs. 'Nothing, son. But tell me. Do you always go
to bed with your pen in your pyjama pocket?'

Tuesday was always a popular day with our class,
because it was Topic Day. And since our latest project
happened to be 'King Arthur's Britain', everyone in
our gang was feeling enthusiastic. We spent most of
the morning writing stories about dragons, and most
of the afternoon exploring the school library for books
about castles and crusades.

Mr Milner had even plucked up the courage to borrow the computer, so we were also taking it in turns to have a go at the Haunted Dungeon program.

'This is brilliant,' said Lanky, when our names were called. 'Best topic we've ever done.'

'Certainly beats Nature Study,' said Gary One. 'I was really sick of leaves and squirrels.'

I knew exactly what he meant. Most of our teachers had spent the Autumn Term studying trees, and splattering the classroom walls with thousands of leaf rubbings. Hibernation and migration can get really boring after a few years, and we were all glad to be doing something different.

Lanky and I pressed a few buttons on the computer keyboard, and ended up being trapped in a secret tunnel, soaked in boiling oil and thrown in the moat. It was terrific.

Jenny and her friend Tracey were next in the queue, and they were dying to get started. 'Move over, your majesty,' said Jenny in a superior sort of tone. 'Looks like you're in a spot of bother here, but don't worry about it. Here come a couple of fair maidens to the rescue.'

Actually, neither of them looked particularly fair to me. In fact, Tracey looks more like an all-in wrestler than a fragile damsel. But I didn't want to upset either of them before the Round Table meeting, so I let Jenny take my place in front of the screen, and then got straight back to the pile of books I had collected.

I was reading about the way real knights had to do their training. They had to practise for hours every day, tilting at a thing called a quintain and learning to fight with both hands in case their sword arm got wounded in battle. I started to draw a series of pictures in my Topic Book, but I didn't have time to finish because we had to clear everything away for the afternoon story session.

We had all made more clutter than usual, so Mr Milner didn't have very long, but he still managed to squash in a short episode about the Round Table.

Apparently, Merlin gave it to Arthur as a surprise present, to stop the knights arguing about where they should sit. A circle doesn't have a top or a bottom, of course, so that solved the problem, and everyone's place was named in gold letters. The seats were called 'Sieges', and some of them were left empty, waiting for knights who hadn't been born yet like Sir Galahad.

Merlin pointed to one of the gaps, and said it was to be known as 'The Siege Perilous', because only the most perfect knight in the land could sit there without dropping dead on the spot. Which seemed a bit drastic if you ask me. Anyway, then Arthur gave his knights the rules of chivalry, and told them to perform good deeds whenever they got the chance. The main thing was that no one could be a knight of the Round Table until he had proved himself worthy of the honour. So everyone had to go away and search for an adventure.

At that point the school bell rang, and Mr Milner removed his spectacles. He blinked for a few seconds to focus his eyes, then he said, 'But Merlin bade farewell to all his friends, and turned to leave with the Enchantress Nimue, who had come from the lake of Avalon. For he was to sleep a long sleep, until once again the world should have need of him.'

With that, he closed the book and yawned deeply,

like someone who had just woken up from a pleasant dream. To me, he looked more like an ancient magician than ever, with his crinkled face and his bony fingers. I wondered whether anyone else had realized who their teacher really was, but the others were just grabbing their bags as usual.

I wanted to say something to him. Something to show him that I understood. I had been trying all day, but it had been impossible to speak to him alone, and now I found I was completely tongue-tied. So all I managed was, 'Good night, Mr Milner,' as I headed for the door.

'Good night, my boy,' he said. And then, in a softer voice, 'Defend the right.'

'What was all that about?' asked Lanky, who had been waiting for me. 'I reckon old Milner's cracking up. Must be old age.'

'Mmm,' I said. There wasn't any point trying to go into details with Lanky.

'It gets people like that,' he went on as we hurried out of the building. 'Old age. Makes them go funny in the head.'

'Not always,' argued Jenny, who was running along backwards to talk to us. 'Sometimes it makes people wise.'

'What about your two aunties?' I said, to be awkward. 'They're both mad aren't they?'

She knew I was only teasing her, so she kept as cool as she could. 'No they're not,' she said. 'They're just eccentric, that's all.'

'What's eccentric mean?' asked Lanky, helping me to steer the chair down the grassy slope.

'It's a polite way to say mad,' I told him, and

giggled while Jenny thumped the top of my head with her pencil case. 'Gerroff. I'm only joking,' I spluttered, then pointed across the pond. 'Anyway, they look as mad as hatters to me.'

The two old ladies were sloshing about in the shallows, and using garden rakes to scrape up all the slime and rotting leaves from the surface of the water. They were both wearing long, flappy white cardigans over their usual white skirts, and they were clumping around in enormous rubber boots.

'Hello, Jennifer, my dear,' they called together. 'Had a good day at school?'

'Yes thanks, Aunt Ava, Aunt Lonnie,' Jenny called back. 'What are you doing?'

'Clearing a space for the moon,' answered the first old lady.

'Making an island of beauty,' answered the second. And they tramped away again, carrying the bucket of weeds and rubbish they had collected.

'Back soon for more,' they called. 'Back soon.' And they staggered off, up the steep path to Morgan's Folly.

They certainly seemed mad to me, but I could tell that Jenny was feeling embarrassed, so I didn't make any rude comments. In any case, the rest of the gang were arriving, so we went to meet them under the oak tree, and I fished a list of names out of my bag.

'OK,' I said. 'First of all, we'd better sit round the tree.'

This was a lot easier said than done. If they all sat on the picnic bench itself with their backs to the trunk, everyone would be facing in different directions. If they all sat on the ground and used the bench for a table, they would only be able to see the tree trunk.

'And I'm not sitting in the mud,' said Perry. 'I'll get my trousers all messy and my mum'll go barmy.'

So in the end, they all dumped their bags on the ground, and perched on those instead. It wasn't a perfect arrangement, but at least we were in a circle.

'OK,' I said again. 'I'll tell you your new names. The three Garys are Gawain, Gareth and Gaheris. Perry can be Percival, Alan can be Agravain, and Lanky can be Lancelot. The girls are Isolde and Elaine. Oh, and Jenny is Queen Guinevere.' I had saved that bit for last, to give her a surprise. I thought she would be really pleased. I mean, Guinevere is a star part.

Immediately there was an explosion of fury from Jenny and her crowd, and I guessed I must have made a mistake somewhere. 'We don't want to be soppy maidens,' Jenny yelled. 'We want to be proper knights and have adventures like everyone else.'

'OK, OK,' I said hurriedly. I could tell I was outnumbered, and I certainly didn't want to risk an argument with Tracey. 'You can choose your own names then. There's plenty left. Balyn and Tristram and Bedivere and all that lot. But I still think Jenny ought to be Guinevere, because it's the same word really.' I couldn't see her reaction, because the tree was in the way, so I just hoped for the best and went on.

'We'll all meet here again tomorrow, and if anyone's managed to perform a deed of chivalry, I'll make them into an official knight of the Round Table.'

That was the end of the first meeting, because

everyone was getting fidgety, and the Garys wanted to collect some more conkers ready for our tournament. So I wrote down the names the girls had chosen. Tracey was to be Tristram, and Lynn had decided on Balyn. They were both in a good mood now, and cantered off home riding imaginary horses.

Only Jenny stayed behind, glowering at me as I altered the list. 'I don't want to be rotten Guinevere,' she said. 'All she ever does is marry Arthur and kiss Lancelot. I've seen the film. So you can forget it.'

'Oh, come on, Jen,' I said, trying to look irresistible. 'Guinevere means the same as Jennifer, so you haven't really got any choice.' That was the wrong thing to say, but it was too late now.

'Oh yes I have got a choice,' she bellowed down my ear. 'If I can't be a knight, then I'll be something else and see how you like it. I'll be Morgana Le Fay. I'm a Morgan, don't forget, so that's more like my name than boring old Guinevere. I'll be your arch enemy, and serve you right too.'

She was red in the face now, and before I could get a word in sideways, she carried straight on. 'In any case, this is a stupid game. How can you be King Arthur? He's been dead for about two thousand years.'

'How do you know?' I demanded. 'Perhaps he's just sleeping, like Merlin. Perhaps he's going to come back when his country needs him.'

'Well then, he wouldn't come back looking like you, would he?' I don't think she meant to hurt my feelings. She was just saying what she thought. 'He'd be a grown-up with a beard, and he'd be riding a big white horse, not a rattly old wheelchair.'

'I bet he wouldn't,' I told her. I had already

wondered about this problem myself, so I had an answer prepared. 'I bet he'd want to come in a really good disguise, like a secret investigator, so his enemies couldn't recognise him, I mean, he could hardly go clanking about the place in a suit of armour, could he? They'd lock him up straight away.'

That shut her up for a minute, but she wasn't likely to admit defeat too easily. Jenny always liked to have the last word. This time, she pointed at Excalibur, which was still lying in my lap on top of the Round Table register.

'Well, what about your silly pen then?' she sniped. 'It's not really special, you know. It's not enchanted or anything like that. It would have to rise up out of the water like Arthur's sword, wouldn't it?'

I didn't want to give in, but I had a nasty feeling she was right. I was remembering the part of the story where Merlin took Arthur to the shores of the lake, and an arm dressed in white samite lifted Excalibur into the air. I looked at my pen moodily, and tried to think of something clever to say, but all I came out with was, 'Well, what is white samite anyway?'

For some reason, that made Jenny grin, and I'm sure she was about to call a truce. But she never got the chance, because two seconds later everything went crazy. Someone yelled, someone else screamed, there was a screech of brakes, a bell ringing, and a sickening thump in the back of my chair. I lurched forwards helplessly, and felt myself toppling towards the slimy surface of the pond.

Just as I thought I was bound to fall, Lanky dropped the handful of conkers he had brought to show me and made a grab for my shoulders. At the same time, Jenny hauled on the handles of my chair, and dragged me back to safety.

'You all right?' asked Lanky. He hadn't moved so fast for years.

'Think so,' I said. 'Just a bit winded, where the seat belt caught me.'

'Oh my God, I'm terribly sorry.' A voice came from somewhere near my feet, and when I looked down I saw it was the Badger Man. He was covered in mud and leaves, and extremely flustered. He staggered to his feet and made a feeble attempt to brush some of the slime off his trousers. 'The bike went out of control,' he explained. 'I was going to ask your friends to sign my petition, but I was going too fast and my tyres skidded on the slope. I didn't hurt you, did I?'

'No,' I assured him, although I was still a bit shaken. 'I'm OK. I was wearing my belt, and the brakes are pretty good on this thing.'

'Thank goodness for that,' he said. 'No real damage done then?'

'I don't think so,' I said. Actually, I was beginning to enjoy the situation, because the Garys had come running over now to soak up the excitement, and I was the centre of attention. But then I saw my piece of paper floating out into the middle of the pond, and I suddenly felt sick.

'What's up, Art?' asked Lanky. 'You've gone all shaky.'

'Perhaps he's suffering from shock,' said Jenny.

'No I'm not,' I croaked. 'It's my pen Excalibur. It's gone.'

'Don't be daft,' said Jenny. 'It can't be far away. It was here a minute ago.'

But we all knew what had happened, and where it was. Buried under the green slime of the village pond. I have to admit I was nearly in tears. I'd promised Mr Milner I would take good care of that pen, and I had lost it already.

'Yoo hoo.' A thin, warbly sound reached us from the far side of the pond. It was one of Jenny's mad aunties. Aunt Ava or Aunt Lonnie, I'm not sure which. 'We saw what happened,' she fluted. 'Is everyone all right?'

'Yes thanks,' shouted Jenny. 'But poor old Adam's lost his best pen. It fell in the water.'

'Not to worry,' the voice warbled back. 'I'll be right over.' And she marched straight into the pond, just like that. Her boots were so tall that they just cleared the surface, and she sloshed across cheerfully, carrying her rake and bucket. 'Now, where shall I hunt?' she asked, when she came to the shallower part.

We all pointed vaguely, and she scraped away enthusiastically under the weeds. I held my breath, and hoped she wasn't burying my pen even deeper in the mud. But after about three wasted attempts, something solid clattered into her bucket. I was afraid it would just be a stone, but she rolled up the sleeves of her grubby white cardigan, and raised Excalibur high in the air.

'Jubilation,' she cried. 'Safe and sound. All's well that ends well.' And she threw it so that it landed perfectly in my lap.

'Thanks,' I said in a squeaky voice, and I watched her as she waded cheerfully back to her own bank.

The Garys waited until the fun was over, then they

hurried away home, leaving us in a stunned group beside the pond.

'Well,' said the Badger Man to break the silence. 'I'd better be going too. I've got so much to organise. So much to do. Letters and petitions and phone calls. If only I could find an otter or a beaver, we might be in the clear.'

'Pardon?' I said, coming out of my daze. 'Why do you want to find an otter?'

'Because it's an endangered species,' he said, as though the answer was obvious. 'People wouldn't be allowed to build houses here if it was a proper nature reserve. There's a law about that sort of thing. So all I need is a rare animal, and the battle's won.' And dragging his bike out of a mound of leaves, he squelched up the slope to the path.

'I'll have to go, too,' said Lanky. 'D'you want a push?'

'Thanks,' I said. 'Are you coming, Jen?'

She was still staring at the pond, and she hadn't said a word for ages. Now, she turned and looked at me. Her face was all crinkly and thoughtful. 'Hm,' she said. And that was all.

She followed us as far as the rectory gates, then wandered off along the High Street by herself, towing her school bag behind her in the dust.

'What's up with her?' asked Lanky. 'Does she still want to be one of the knights?'

'Expect so,' I said. But I knew there was more to it than that. Jenny and I had been friends for a long time, and we understood each other very well. Too well sometimes. So I was quite sure she had seen everything as clearly as I had done.

The Badger Man had played the part of mad Sir Pellinore. First he had lost my pen, and then he had gone away in search of a Questing Beast. But best of all had been the sight of Excalibur rising up out of the water like magic, and held up by a mysterious arm clothed in white samite. Well, white wool anyway.

So there couldn't be any argument now. I was definitely King Arthur. I just hoped that Jenny would see sense, and change her mind about being my arch enemy. Morgana Le Fay.

4 Morgana

'Why do they call him the Badger Man?' Lanky asked next morning, when we were waiting for the school doors to open.

'But everyone knows that,' I said. Honestly, sometimes I think Lanky goes round with a paper bag on his head half the time.

Jenny had been leaning against the wall pretending to ignore us, but she couldn't resist an opportunity to give Lanky a lecture. 'Because he studies badgers, of course,' she said. 'He's always writing about the local animals. You must have seen him. Sometimes he sits up all night making notes and taking photos with a special camera.'

'Well, I've never noticed.' Lanky took off his glasses and fiddled with the strip of sticking plaster that held the two halves together. When he had finished, the lenses were all smudged and greasy. No wonder he went round in a world of his own. 'Is he famous then?' he went on. 'What do his books look like? Are they any good?'

'Dunno,' said Jenny. 'No one's ever seen them. I don't think he's had any printed yet.'

'But he's really clever,' I chipped in. I wanted to whip up some support for the Badger Man, because he seemed an interesting sort of person to me, with his old bike and his backpack and his pockets full of toadstools. 'He's been to university and everything. And now he's organising a petition to save the village pond. We've all signed it. Dad and Kit and me.'

'What's happening to the village pond, then?' The three Garys had just arrived, so I explained what I knew, which wasn't much.

'Holiday homes?' said Gary One. 'Who wants to come here for their holidays? My mum and dad spend all year saving up so we can get away from this dump.'

'Rich people, I suppose,' I said. 'Looking for a bit of peace and quiet. Getting away from all the traffic in the towns.'

'But if they come here and build houses all over our village, it'll be just as noisy as wherever it is they come from,' said Gary Two.

'Yeah,' said Gary Three. 'So where's the point in that?'

We were all agreed. 'You'll have to sign the Badger Man's petition then,' I said. 'And help to keep the pond tidy. He says we might have a chance if we can prove it's a proper beauty spot. With rare plants and insects and things.'

'A conservation site,' Jenny corrected me. She liked showing off long words.

'It's one of those all right,' said Lanky warmly. 'My mum sits on the picnic benches for hours, nattering to all her friends.'

Everyone groaned. 'Not conversation,' I said. 'Conservation. You know. Wild and natural, like the animal films on the telly.'

Gary One pulled a face. 'In that case, we haven't got a hope,' he said. 'Most people in the village use the pond for a rubbish bin. It's full of old tin cans.'

'My dad takes all his grass cuttings down there, and tips them under the trees,' said Gary Two.

'Yeah,' said Gary Three. 'Everyone does that.'

Then the bell rang, and feeling rather gloomy we all trooped indoors. I pushed my wheels hard to keep up with Jenny. It was a relief to see that she was back to her normal spiky self this morning, and I wanted to keep her in a good mood. Perhaps she would offer to back down, and agree to be Guinevere after all. She hung my jacket up for me, which was a hopeful sign, so I made an effort to please her.

'I suppose your aunties were helping the Badger Man last night,' I said. 'Kind of them, wasn't it?'

'Course it was,' she said snappily. 'I told you they weren't mad. At least they care about this village, which is more than you can say about most people who live here.'

'All right, all right,' I said. 'No need to bite my head off. Are you coming to the Round Table meeting with us tonight?'

'No fear,' she said, looking crosser than ever. 'I've told you already. The only part I'll play in your daft game is Morgana, and that's that.'

'Oh, suit yourself then,' I said. 'See if I care.' And I left her to stand in the cloakroom by herself, muttering rude words at the mirror.

At breaktime, a stiff wind was blowing, so I huddled into the wheelchair, holding my jacket round myself to keep warm. It was October now, and there were leaves flying about the field in orange whirlpools. I could feel my nose turning red, so I steered my wheels towards the bike shelter where I could watch the others without freezing to death.

Lanky came with me, and sat down to lean his back against my armrest. We munched our way through a bag of stale crisps that the tuck shop had sold us at half price, and we didn't speak until we had sucked the last clinging fragments from our teeth.

Finally Lanky said, 'I don't know what to do, Art.' He sounded really troubled, as if he had some life-or-death problem on his mind.

'Don't worry about it, Lanky,' I said. 'Just sign the petition with the rest of us, and ask your parents to keep the pond tidy.'

He twisted round to look at me blankly, then said, 'I don't mean that. It's the brave deed that's bothering me. Where am I going to find a dragon to kill or a damsel to rescue? If I'm supposed to be Lancelot, I'll have to do something pretty amazing before the meeting tonight.'

'No problem,' I said. 'You've already done it.'

'I have?' He stood up to brush the crisp crumbs off his trousers, but his face looked blanker than ever.

'Yes,' I insisted. 'You remember. Last night, when you saved my life.'

'Who me? When did I do that?'

'When you stopped me from falling in the pond. I could've drowned if I'd landed with my face in the mud, but you and Jenny rescued me, didn't you? So that means you saved the life of the King, and I reckon that must count as a first class good deed.'

'I suppose it must.' Lanky sounded quite impressed with himself now, and he certainly looked a lot happier. He ambled over to the side of the shelter, and gazed out at the world for a few moments. Something had caught his eye, and I found myself watching too.

At first, all I spotted was Jenny, racing across the field and waving her arms in the air. She was easy to recognize because she was wearing a bouncy white bobble hat her aunties had knitted for her. But then I was distracted by the sight of a violent argument that had broken out near the far gate. Every so often the wind would toss an odd, angry word in our direction, and I could tell things were beginning to get out of hand.

'Who is it?' asked Lanky.

'Perry and Alan, I think,' I said. 'But I don't know who they're shouting at. It looks like a parent to me. Anyway, Miss Lane's just clomping over to sort it out.' The duty teacher was obviously furious, and I was glad I wouldn't be at the receiving end of her bad temper. Miss Lane was definitely the school's resident dragon.

'What's she saying?' Lanky was frantically wiping his glasses on his anorak.

'How should I know?' I answered irritably. I didn't much care. I was too concerned about my own problems. 'Anyway, what about me?' I demanded. 'It's all right for you. You're only a knight. But I'm the King, and I ought to be doing the bravest deed of all.'

Lanky nodded sympathetically, but I could tell his mind was on other things. Once more, the white bobble hat flashed past the shelter, and as it did so, a frantic yapping noise drew our attention towards the school dustbins. A terrified bundle of scruffy fur was being chased by a crowd of boys, who were flapping their coats like a tribe of demented matadors after a bull.

'I think they've caught him,' said Lanky, squinting through his clouded lenses. 'No. Hang about. He's escaped between Gary's legs. Now the other two Garys are dodging round the games hut to head him off. Oh, and now Miss Lane's blowing her whistle at them. She looks just like King Kong, doesn't she?'

'Mmm,' I said, even more irritably than before. 'Come on, Lanky. Think. Give me an idea.' Mind you, I don't know why I bothered to ask. Bright ideas aren't exactly Lanky's trade mark. But I was so desperate, I was ready to try anything. I'd been awake half the night worrying, and by now my brain felt completely scrambled.

I looked at my friend hopefully, but he was watching the white bobble hat again. This time, a procession of little girls in neat blue uniforms was winding its way up the school path, led by a nun whose skirts flapped wildly in the breeze. Jenny darted off in the opposite direction, but two girls sprang forwards and stood on the path barring the way. They seemed to be chanting some sort of rhyme, and the nun threw up her hands in horror. Then Miss Lane rushed up with a dog under her arm, and said something which shocked the nun even more.

'What did you say?' asked Lanky vaguely.

'An idea.' I was practically shouting at him now. 'What am I going to do? Can't you think of anything?'

Lanky wrinkled up his face in a supreme effort, opened his mouth to speak, took a deep breath, then closed his mouth again.

This was hopeless. I began to tug at my wheels, so that the chair rumbled out of the shelter. 'Thanks very much,' I said sourly. 'Thanks for nothing.'

The bell was due to ring at any moment, and I had just wasted an entire breaktime. I could hear Lanky's voice behind me, but I pretended I had the wind in my ears and ignored him. I was the first in the queue when Miss Lane opened the doors, and the first person back in the classroom.

I sat at my desk waiting for the others, and grumbling to myself in the silence. I was going to look a proper fool at the Round Table meeting, and because I was in such a bad mood, I decided it was all Lanky's fault. I knew I wasn't being fair, but I really was rattled.

Then I was shaken out of myself by a loud noise coming from the corridor. I span my chair round to watch, as the rest of the class burst into the room like a herd of angry football supporters after an own goal.

'What's up?' I asked as Tracey and Lynn flounced past and threw themselves into their seats.

'Mouldy old Miss Lane making a fuss as usual,' growled Tracey. 'We were only protecting our island fortress from the invading hordes.'

'Well, we were only rescuing a damsel in distress from the clutches of a cruel giant,' said Perry.

'And we were only storming the monster in his lair.' said Gary One.

'That's all the thanks you get for risking your lives,' said Gary Two.

'Yeah,' said Gary Three. 'Some people are never grateful. It's not fair.'

The only person who didn't seem at all concerned

was Jenny. She slid past my desk really quietly, and when she sat down I couldn't help noticing the look of triumph on her face. But there wasn't time to ask any more questions, because Mr Milner was at the door now, looking rather crumpled and dejected.

'What on earth has been going on?' he asked weakly. 'It's always the same in windy weather. You all seem to go totally wild. I have never heard so many complaints in all my life. And as for poor Miss Lane. She's absolutely worn out, and now she's got to go and teach her class. Has anyone got an explanation for me?'

His tired eyes studied each face in turn, and most of the class began to fidget in an embarrassed way. We all knew he was waiting for confessions and apologies, but no one wanted to be the first to speak. I knew I was innocent, but in the end I just couldn't stand the tension any longer.

'Please, Mr Milner,' I said shyly. 'I don't think anyone meant to annoy you. They were just trying to perform their deeds of chivalry. You know. Like the Knights of the Round Table, in the story.'

Mr Milner's face went one shade paler, and he slumped against the class draining board with a groan. 'You mean they've managed to upset one teacher, one parent, one unfortunate puppy and a whole coachload of visiting netball players, all in the course of one short playtime. And all because they were trying to do acts of goodness?' he muttered in a daze. 'Well, Heaven help us if they ever decide to go out and cause trouble.'

He produced a scrap of torn computer paper from his jacket pocket, and called out a list of names. 'Perry and Alan. Gary, Gary and Gary.' Somehow he managed to make the three names all sound completely different. 'Tracey and Lynn.' The rest of the class breathed sighs of relief, as he wandered over to his desk. His shoulders were sagging, and I noticed that his jacket seemed far too big for him. Either that, or he had shrunk.

'All right,' he said. 'Why would two knights in shining armour want to attack a small first year, and then shout abuse at her aunty.'

Perry and Alan started to make squeaking noises, and Alan's ears went the colour of dried ketchup. 'We didn't, sir, honest,' Perry began. Then he cleared his throat and tried to speak more normally. 'We thought we were rescuing the little kid from a dangerous enemy. This big fat woman in a green coat started dragging her out of the playground, so we ran over to help, didn't we, Alan?'

Alan nodded, but said nothing to help his friend, so Perry had to carry on by himself. 'The kid was crying her eyes out, so we asked her if it was her mum, and she said no. So we tried to rescue her, didn't we, Alan?'

Alan nodded again, but we could all see he was too nervous to speak, so Perry sighed and went on. 'We didn't know, sir. No one told us the fat lady was her aunty. We thought she was an evil green giant or something.' He looked at Alan for help, then shrugged and concentrated on his own feet. 'Sorry, sir,' he added in a voice so small we could hardly hear him.

We were all dying to know exactly what he had shouted at the fat lady. Most of us had a pretty good idea. Perry's big brother used to teach him some incredible words. Enough to make your toes curl. No wonder Mr Milner was looking like the chief undertaker at his own funeral.

At the end of Perry's story, he sat on the edge of his desk and made a whimpering sound. 'Foolish children,' he murmured. Then in a louder voice, he added, 'The child was crying because she had a bad toothache, and she didn't want to go to the dentist. I'm quite sure her poor aunty had enough troubles, without any extra help from you.'

He made several little clicking noises with his tongue, then directed his attention towards the three Garys. 'Well?' he said. 'Why did you spend your breaktime tormenting a poor little puppy, until Miss Lane had to rescue it from underneath the games hut?'

'It was a trespasser, sir,' began Gary One. 'I mean, dogs aren't allowed in the playground, are they, sir? We were just trying to round it up for you.'

'It could have turned vicious,' went on Gary Two. 'It was only small, but it didn't half have sharp teeth. It could easily have attacked a first year and given him lockjaw or something. That's what stray dogs do.'

'Yeah,' said Gary Three. 'They're dangerous, dogs are. We reckoned it was a monster, so we went to capture it. And we didn't have any armour or weapons or anything. We were being brave, sir.'

This time, Mr Milner whimpered out loud. 'That animal is a valuable pedigree Samoyed. It belongs to the headmistress of the Infants School, and she had only let it out for two minutes so it could answer the call of nature. She couldn't believe her eyes when she saw what was going on. If it hadn't been for Miss

Lane, you boys would have been reported to the RSPCA by now.'

He rubbed his hands over his face, to rearrange the wrinkles, and then began again. 'Tracey. I don't suppose you also have a perfectly reasonable explanation, do you? Tell me. Why did you and your friend decide to insult a party of visitors, who had just arrived for a friendly match with the third years?'

Tracey stood up very cautiously and scratched her ear. We could almost hear her brain ticking over. When she spoke, her voice was gruff and low. 'We didn't know they were friends. We thought they were the enemy. I think we might have got a bit carried away, sir. Sorry.' And she sat down heavily, blowing air through her teeth.

Mr Milner nodded and smiled grimly. 'You got carried away,' he repeated. 'You're sorry. I should just hope you would be sorry. All of you. I have never heard anything so disgraceful in my whole teaching career. Now, what I want to know is . . .' (I was sure he was speaking to me) '. . . who put you up to all this? Who put the idea in your heads?'

We all stared back at him, feeling a bit baffled. After all, to be fair, it was his own fault. He was the one who told us the King Arthur stories in the first place. But of course, we couldn't say that, could we?

I took a deep breath and put my hand up. 'Mr Milner,' I said carefully, 'it was me. I started it. I told everyone they had to do a brave deed if they wanted to be in my Round Table gang. So I suppose I'm the one to blame.'

He looked at me as though I had just hit him between the eyes with a wet bath sponge. 'You?' he said softly. 'Of all people? What made you do it, Art? Why did you lead your friends into bad ways like that?'

What could I say? I didn't think this was the right time to start explaining about Pendragon and Excalibur and Sir Pellinore, so I just sat there, waiting for him to explode. Perhaps he would use his magic powers at last, and turn me into a grain of salt or something like that.

He didn't. He stared at me long and hard for what seemed like hours, then suddenly, for no apparent reason, burst out laughing. 'Brave deeds,' he gurgled. 'Acts of Chivalry. Bless my soul, poor Miss Lane. Oh dear, oh dear, oh dear.' And he collapsed in his chair, mopping at his eyes with the chalky duster.

When he had recovered himself enough to speak, he leaned forwards with his elbows on the register and said, 'Well, just spare us the good deeds in future, won't you? Go back to being your normal, revolting selves. Life's much more peaceful that way.' Then he was off again, giggling into his hand like an excited first year.

We gaped at each other, and raised our eyebrows questioningly. Surely he was going to punish us? Keep us all in for the rest of the week and cancel our games lessons till the end of term? That sort of thing.

We waited, but nothing happened. All he did was to tell us to get out our work, and try not to do any more good deeds before lunchtime. We couldn't believe our luck. Alan and Perry had certainly been expecting the worst. Letters home, and a temporary expulsion for bad language, at the very least.

'Thanks for saving us,' Perry whispered to me as he

squeezed past my desk to fetch the click wheel. 'I don't know how you did it, but you certainly saved our skins. My mum would have gone berserk if she'd found out what I said to that lady.'

In fact, I was incredibly popular for the rest of the morning. People kept patting me on the shoulders, or nudging me in the arm every time they went by, and Gary One even passed me one of the free fizzy scrunchers he gets from his dad's shop. As a result, I was feeling so confident that I decided to take a risk and ask Mr Milner a question.

When the bell rang, I hung around putting my books away and scraping pencil shavings on to a piece of paper. Then I wheeled myself over to the litter-bin next to Mr Milner's desk. He was marking a pile of topic books, but his shoulders kept quivering as though he was still enjoying a private joke.

'Mr Milner,' I said, feeling rather awkward now that we were alone. Perhaps it would be wiser to ask an ordinary question first, before I got on to the subject of Merlin. He looked up, so I took that as an invitation and went on. 'Is everything going to be all right now? I mean, what about the little girl's aunty, and the Headmistress, and the netball team? And Miss Lane? Won't they all expect us to be punished?'

'What for?' He was smiling properly now, so that his eyes crinkled up at the corners. 'How can I punish you for doing good deeds? Rescuing maidens in distress. Defending the school from savage beasts and invading armies. That wouldn't be right, would it?'

I knew he was teasing me, and my courage drifted away. I couldn't talk about King Arthur if he was only going to start laughing again. I took off my brake, and began to turn my chair towards the door, but a quiet cough made me look back.

His face was quite serious now, and very kindly. 'Don't worry, Art,' he said. 'I'll sort out Miss Lane for you. And all the others. I have my ways, you know. But make sure your knights do something really useful next time, won't you? If you're going to be a leader, you must learn to lead people in the right direction. Not push them into trouble.'

I nodded. I could feel his pale eyes reading my thoughts, and my tongue dried in my mouth. I was sure now that Mr Milner understood everything about me, and knew exactly what I was trying to do. 'Thank you, sir,' I mumbled. Then I clattered away into the corridor, and hurried off to join the others in the canteen queue.

But as it turned out, we didn't get off entirely scot-free, because that afternoon Mr Milner decided to give the King Arthur project a rest, and teach us a seasonal lesson instead. 'Autumn' he wrote on the board. 'Hibernation and Migration.' He couldn't have thought of a better punishment. I felt like crawling into a hole and hibernating myself.

Fancy Mr Milner letting us down like that. In no time, everyone was chattering happily about robins and swallows and hedgehogs, or writing poems about fluttering leaves. I sat with Excalibur between my fingers, facing my blank paper in despair. I couldn't think of a single thing to say. Or at least, nothing that I hadn't already said a thousand times before.

All around me, children were writing furiously. Apart from Lanky, that is, who was trying to fit a cartridge in his pen, and sploshing drops of ink into the litter bin. I desperately wanted to please Mr Milner, after everything that had happened, but it was no use. I was absolutely stuck.

'Nothing to say, Art?' He was standing behind me, inspecting my empty page.

'No,' I said. 'Sorry. I'm just not very interested in nature study. It's boring.'

'Well, you do surprise me,' he said. 'I thought you were a friend of the Badger Man. And didn't I hear you talking about the village pond?'

'Mmm, yes,' I admitted. 'But that's different. I mean, that's conservation, isn't it?'

He chuckled. 'Precisely,' he said. 'So why don't you write about that? Tell me how you feel about the builders, and what they'll be doing to your meeting place.'

That idea certainly did the trick. I started writing at top speed, pouring out all my thoughts about the pond and the horse chestnut trees. But most of all about the big oak. My tree, with its sheltering branches and circular seat. I said how important it was, not only to me and the people in the village, but to the animals as well. The birds and the squirrels and the insects that relied on it for their homes or their food.

I explained how the pond was used by the local children for paddling and fishing with jam jars. How it was a hiding place for beetles and caddis-fly larvae. How it was a bath tub for passing ducks and village sparrows. How the village would never be the same without it.

'We don't mind new people coming to live here,' I finished. 'So long as they don't spoil all the best bits.

If they drain our pond and cover it in concrete, they might just as well stay in their rotten towns. But if we all do what the Badger Man says and take care of the pond, it could be the most valuable thing in the village. A proper conservation area. And I think the new people would much rather have that, than boring old concrete.'

I would have written more, but I suddenly became aware that the bell was ringing, and the afternoon had disappeared. I had been so busy, I hadn't even noticed. Mr Milner stopped at my desk to collect my work, and I handed him three sheets of paper, totally covered in thick black writing.

'It must be Excalibur,' I said. 'I've never written as much as this in my whole life.'

He nodded, and I could tell he was pleased. 'Well done, Art,' he said. 'I'll look forward to marking this.' And he put it with the rest of the papers into his carrier bag.

It was only then that I realized we had missed our usual story session. 'You will tell us some more about King Arthur, won't you?' I said as I prepared to leave. 'I want to know the end of the story.'

He started to laugh again. 'Tomorrow's another day,' he said. 'Go on. Be off with you.' And I hurried off to meet Lanky in the cloakroom.

We all arrived at the pond as planned, but some of the others were looking a bit subdued. Only Lanky seemed reasonably pleased with himself, as I summoned them to the Round Table.

'Percival and Agravaine,' I called. 'Gawain, Gareth and Gaheris. Tristan, Balyn and Lancelot.' One by one they stood up to announce what deeds they had accomplished, and it was at that point I noticed there was an empty place. 'Where's Jenny?' I asked. 'I mean Guinevere. She should be here, sitting next to me, now she's supposed to be the Queen.'

'Dunno,' said Perry. 'Haven't spoken to her since breaktime. When she came up and told us about the fat lady.'

'That's right,' said Alan. 'She said there was a spot of bother we ought to sort out, and then she ran off.'

'Yeah,' said Gary Three. 'She came over and told us there was a mad dog biting the little kids, and we didn't see her after that.'

'She told us to shout at the netball bus,' said Tracey. 'She said St Winifred's were a load of lousy cheats, and they'd only come to smash our team into the ground. But we didn't see her after that, did we, Lynn?'

'No,' said Lynn darkly. 'She hasn't come near me since. She ate her dinner with the girls from Miss Lane's class, and then she worked in the quiet corner all afternoon.'

A general murmur of suspicion ran round the circle. Everyone began to talk about Jenny as though she were a spy or a sinister enemy. I couldn't help overhearing the whispered comments, but I kept my private opinions to myself. This wasn't the best time to mention the damning evidence I had witnessed at breaktime. The sight of Jenny's white bobble hat darting from incident to incident, and the smug expression on her face as she followed the others into class. But inside my head, I heard again the threat she had made me last night.

'If I can't be a knight, then I'll be something else

and see how you like it. I'll be Morgana Le Fay. I'll be your arch enemy, and serve you right too.' Trust Jenny to keep her word.

I brought my hands down hard against the arms of my chair to call attention, and Perry obligingly blew a fanfare. 'All right,' I called. 'Forget about Jenny. We need an empty seat anyway, for the Siege Perilous. From now on, no one is allowed to sit in that place, because it's reserved for Sir Galahad. And now for the grand ceremony. I'm going to make you all proper knights of the Round Table.'

They all lined up and took it in turns to bow in front of me, while I performed the 'Once-Twice-Thrice' routine, using Excalibur instead of a sword. But just as I was getting ready to do the big speech I had prepared, a voice yelled out, 'What about weedy old King Arthur, then? What brave and fearless deed did he do today?'

It was unmistakably Jenny, but I couldn't see her. I span my chair to get a good view of the whole site, but there was no sign of the bobble hat anywhere. I could feel myself growing hot with embarrassment. 'Where are you?' I shouted. 'Why won't you stop messing about, and come and be Queen Guinevere?'

'No thanks,' came the voice. 'Forget it. I don't want to play your stupid games anyway.'

There was a loud rustling noise just above my head, and to our surprise, Jenny scrambled out of the branches of the oak tree and landed beside my chair. 'You haven't answered my question yet, your majesty,' she said sarcastically, making an elaborate bow. 'What wondrous act of chivalry did you perform this day?'

'He saved us all from the school dragon, that's what.' Lanky had rushed across to stand behind me, and I suddenly remembered why he was my best friend. 'If it hadn't been for Art, Miss Lane would have had the lot of us for dinner.'

That was the signal for the others to move too. 'Let's get her,' shouted Gary One. 'Scrag her. She got us all into trouble. She nearly got us thrown out of the school.'

'And reported to the RSPCA,' added Gary Two.

'Yeah,' bellowed Gary Three. 'Charge.'

Jenny dodged out of his way, sprinted a few yards and turned to blow a raspberry at them. 'Go on then. Scrag me. If you can catch me.' And she was away up the slope before anyone could grab her.

Gary Two made a dash for the trees, to head her off, but I didn't want the meeting to end in a shambles, so I yelled after him. 'Let her go. She's not worth the bother.'

I waited for everyone to get back into their places, more or less, and then gave a few coughs to show I was ready to make my speech. It was a waste of time. No one was in the mood to listen to it now. So instead I just made a quick announcement.

'At the next meeting, we'll make the final plans for our great tournament, to find the best and bravest knight in the land. But for now, remember you must always uphold the good and protect the weak.'

'Fat lot of good that is,' Perry muttered, but I carried on anyway.

'Our mission is to save the village pond. We shall join with the Badger Man to ward off the forces of evil, and protect our sacred lake from the enemy.'

They liked that. I must admit, it sounded quite effective, and I wasn't surprised when some of them cheered.

As they picked up their bags to leave, Alan said, 'What sort of thing d'you have in mind? My mum won't let me stay up and guard the pond all night. I have to go to bed after the News, or she gets really ratty.'

'Mmm,' I said. 'Well, I'm not really sure what we're doing yet. We'll talk about it tomorrow.' Then Lanky and I left the others to collect more conkers, while we made our way home.

'What's the matter with Jenny?' he asked as we parted. 'She's never been as moody as this before.'

'I don't think she is being moody,' I said. 'I think she's being Morgana.' And I left him to puzzle that one out by himself, because I was in a hurry to get indoors. I had noticed the Badger Man's bike leaning against our wall, and I guessed he would be in the kitchen having a chat with Mum. He often stopped for a tea break at the rectory, and I always enjoyed the chance of a talk with him.

That night he was still in a serious mood.

'How's the petition going?' I asked.

'So so,' he said. 'But this is only a small village, and I'll never manage to collect more than a few hundred names, even if everyone signs.'

'Oh,' I said. 'How many do you need then?'

'Thousands, to be any good. And one or two famous people on the list would probably help. But there's no one like that round here. Oh well.' He smiled thinly. 'I'll just have to keep looking for that mythical beast, won't I?'

'Wouldn't a badger do?' I asked. 'I thought they were rare these days, and you've got photos of lots of them.'

'I know,' he said. 'But they all live at the other end of the village, out on private farming land. Not too keen on mud, you see. It makes them rheumaticky. So I'm afraid they're no use to us this time.'

He dived under the table, and pulled a small handbook from his backpack. 'These are the species we're after,' he said, flipping quickly through the pages. 'See. Water-loving creatures. Otters, newts, this little chap.'

I peered at the picture he was tapping, and saw a squashed, knobbly face with sad eyes. 'A frog?' I said. 'I thought they were really common.'

'Not this one,' he explained. 'It's not a frog at all. It's a natterjack toad. But they're more or less impossible to find at this time of year, because they've all started hibernating. Even if there were any there in the first place.'

He stood up with a sigh, and began to wrap himself in his scarves. 'Must be off,' he said. 'Take a few photos of the sunset over Morgan's Folly, before they build houses in the way.' And he hitched his pack on to his shoulders. 'You'd better make the most of those conker trees while you can,' he added. 'I expect they're all for the chop. Even Arthur's Oak. Unless we can stop them.'

'Arthur's Oak?' I repeated. 'I didn't know the big tree was called Arthur's Oak.'

'Oh yes,' said Mum, who had just come in from the garden with a pot of dying geraniums. 'No one seems to know why, but it's certainly very old. It's such a shame to destroy all that history for a few piles of bricks.' She shook her head, and watched through the side window as the Badger Man clambered on his bike.

'Just like a knight in shining armour,' she said dreamily. 'Riding off into the sunset. I do hope he finds whatever it is he's looking for.'

'So do I,' I said. 'So do I.'

5   The Siege Perilous

The next morning, Jenny helped me hang up my jacket, just as though nothing had ever happened.

'I don't get it,' I said. 'Yesterday you were my arch enemy. How come you're back to normal now?'

Jenny gave me a sideways look. 'I'm only Morgana when you play your daft games. And at the moment, you're Adam and I'm Jenny. But if you decide to be Arthur again, and have another Round Table meeting after school, you'd better watch out.' She started to grin, and I could see she was really enjoying herself. 'After all,' she said. 'There's no point being King Arthur if you don't have any battles to fight, is there?'

Which I suppose was true. All the same, I had a lot of trouble persuading the rest of the gang to see her argument.

'She nearly got us boiled in oil,' complained Perry. 'And now she expects us to forget it.'

'No she doesn't,' I tried to explain. 'She just wants us to understand that she was only playing her part in the story. That's all.'

There were a few grudging mumbles of agreement, then Gary One said, 'Fair enough. So long as she realizes we're only playing our parts when we scrag her alive.'

'Yeah,' said Gary Three, sticking a school ruler in his belt, and doing his best to look dangerous.

But since our class had been challenged to a football match at lunchtime, against the third years, it was generally decided to postpone the scragging of Jenny until after school. Well, let's face it, she was the best goalie our class ever had, and we couldn't afford to lose her from the team. Just as well, because we won the game five-nil, and Jenny was definitely back in favour by the time we went indoors again.

We were all on our politest behaviour that day, particularly as we wanted to hear some more of the King Arthur story. It seems we had all managed to please him with our 'Autumn' stories, and he had spent his lunchbreak sticking the best ones on the wall. Of course, I had a look for mine. I was expecting it to be right in the middle somewhere, but to my disappointment it hadn't been chosen. I couldn't think why that should be. I knew it was the longest, neatest piece of work I had ever done. Still, there was no point getting upset about it. I shrugged, and wheeled myself over to my desk.

At least we were back on our King Arthur project again. 'Just as long as you don't get carried away with it all,' Mr Milner warned us. 'I don't want any more trouble like we had yesterday.'

So we all looked as angelic as we could, and he let us spend an hour designing battle shields and banners. My coat of arms was divided into four by a cross, and in each of the quarters I had drawn heraldic symbols. Crowns and swords mainly, as I'm not too good at difficult things like lions and unicorns.

By home time, the basic plan was finished, although

it still needed painting. Lanky had drawn a dragon in the middle of his shield, and made a border of flames round the outside. It looked pretty effective already. 'That's great,' I said. 'We can use these when we hold our great tournament.'

Clearing away all the mess and glue back into the classroom cupboards took us ages, though, and there were only a few minutes left for the story session. But Mr Milner found the book and got himself settled on the radiator anyway.

'I'll just remind you of the beginning of the legend,' he said, 'and I'll leave you to wonder about the ending.'

Then he went over the part where Merlin showed Arthur the Round Table for the first time. There were loads of details I had forgotten, and I sat forward in my chair trying to memorize every word. The bits about the Siege Perilous, for instance, where Merlin says that it's reserved for the purest knight of all. Apparently, Sir Galahad would go riding off to find the Holy Grail, which had been lost for centuries. But at the same time, the knights of the Round Table would all start fighting with each other and the great friendship would end.

This was all thanks to Arthur's enemies, of course. Morgana Le Fay, and a new character who would appear right at the end of the book. An evil, mystery knight whose name was Sir Mordred, and who wanted to destroy everything.

That was the point where the bell rang, and Mr Milner closed the book. He asked us to try to find out something about the Holy Grail before tomorrow's session, and then he let us go.

For some reason, that set us buzzing with silly suggestions. Lanky reckoned a grail must be something like Aladdin's lamp, because that was the only magical thing he could think of. Jenny said it was probably an ancient book, full of spells for raising the dead and stuff like that. Perry said it ought to be something out of the Bible, belonging to Moses or St Peter or some other saint. But as none of us knew what we were talking about, we didn't get any nearer to solving the problem.

We were still discussing it when we reached the village pond. The four of us grouped on the bank and took a break to admire the view while we waited for the rest of the gang to arrive. Everything looked so much tidier now, and thanks to Jenny's mad aunties, the water was clear enough to turn the world upside down. The thick branches of Arthur's Oak reflected darkly amongst the remaining weeds, and an occasional insect set the great tree quivering.

The Badger Man must have collected barrow-loads of junk, because even the litter bins were empty. In fact, it all looked so respectable that Lanky bunged his finished Munchy wrapper in his jacket pocket. Normally, he would have just thrown it on the ground. But then, normally the place looked like a council tip anway, so it was no wonder that nobody cared.

'Looking good, isn't it?' said Perry, swivelling round on his heels. 'Pity about the graffiti, though.'

'What graffiti?' I was bristling with anger as soon as I heard the word. 'If people come down here and start spraying paint all over the seats we'll never be able to stop the builders. They'll say it's just a bit of old waste ground, and not a beauty spot at all.'

I whirled my chair through a half circle, splashing mud up everyone's legs, and inspected the picnic benches. I had expected to see fluorescent swear words, or love hearts splattered all over them, but they looked fine to me. 'What are you talking about, Perry?' I asked. 'I can't see any graffiti.'

'Nor me,' said Jenny. 'Are you trying to wind us up or something?'

'No.' Perry sounded quite affronted. 'And you're a good one to talk, I must say. After all the trouble you caused yesterday.' They both looked ready for a fight.

'I can see it,' Lanky interrupted them happily. Whether he was pleased to spot the paint marks, or glad to stop the argument, I'll never know. But I turned to look where he was pointing, and immediately groaned. I felt quite sick.

'That's not graffiti,' I said dismally. 'That's the builders.' Round the waist of every tree, someone had painted a broad white band. The horse chestnuts, still heavy with green husks. The small birches gathered near the footpath. The willow at the edge of the pond. And worst of all, the great oak itself.

'Oh,' said Perry. 'So that's it then.'

We trailed over to our usual places round the tree, and stared in silence at the damp death-threat. Blobs of white had trickled down the ridges of the bark and dried there like tears. I felt as though someone had just punched me in the stomach. What could we possibly do now?

Before I could get my brain into gear, we heard chattering voices heading towards us, and looked round. The others were slithering down the bank to join us, and were obviously in high spirits. Gary One had shared out a bag of fizzy scrunchers, and the popping sensations had given everyone the giggles.

'My tongue's gone bananas,' announced Lynn, flinging her bag to the ground and sitting on it.

'Have a scruncher, Art,' said Gary, offering me the last few.

'No thanks,' I muttered. 'Not in the mood. Sorry.'

'What's up with you lot then?' asked Gary Two. 'Don't tell me we aren't going to arrange the tournament. I've been looking forward to that.'

'I don't know about the tournament,' I said. 'I reckon we'll have to cancel everything at this rate. Look.' I pointed at the white rings, and everyone gasped.

'But they can't chop the oak tree down,' protested Tracey. 'It's been here hundreds of years. It's not fair.'

'Yes they can,' I said. 'If they can get permission. And it looks as if they have.'

Gary One was thumping his hands together furiously. 'Well, tough luck,' he growled. 'Because no one asked us. And we're not going to let them build their crummy houses here.'

'That's right,' said Gary Two. 'Let's stop them.'

'Yeah,' said Gary Three. 'Let's scrag them.' Which was his answer to most things, but I knew how he felt.

I sighed, and waved my hand for quiet. 'It's not as easy as that,' I said. 'They're grown-ups. We can't just go and punch them on their noses. That wouldn't stop them anyway.'

'Well, why don't we wash the paint off, then?' said Lanky. 'They aren't allowed to chop down trees that haven't been marked.' He looked really pleased with this unusual flash of brilliance, but of course I had to disappoint him.

'No use, Lanky,' I said. 'Even if we could get the trees clean, we'd only slow things up for a couple of days. We'll have to think of something better than that.'

'I reckon we need a miracle,' Jenny shouted down from her perch amongst the branches. She was still refusing to sit with the rest of us, but she didn't intend to miss out on any of the real action. 'You lot ought to go and look for the Holy Grail, or something.'

'Oh, very funny,' grumbled Perry. 'We don't even know what it is, so how can we?'

But before another argument could get started, there was a sudden, unexpected interruption. 'Can I come and be one of your knights, please? Can I?'

The voice was high and squeaky, and it came from somewhere near my right ear. I twisted round, and found myself looking at a small, skinny figure with big ears and even bigger glasses. It was Gavin, Lanky's little brother.

Lanky groaned. 'Push off, Gav. You're too young for this game. First years aren't allowed.' He sounded as fierce as he could, but he knew he was already defeated. Gavin usually got his own way. He was a bouncy sort of person, who played a mean game of Scrabble, and had more brains than anyone else in his family. Which was probably why Lanky wasn't too keen on having him hanging around.

'Don't be daft,' said Gavin, as soon as his brother had finished. 'There's stacks of room. See.' And he plonked himself straight down in the empty space next to me.

'Hey. Watch it,' I began. 'That's the Siege Perilous, you know.' But it was too late. There he was, perched on his school bag, and grinning triumphantly.

'What's a siege perilous?' he asked.

'It's the last empty seat at the Round Table,' I explained, 'and it's reserved for Sir Galahad. If anyone else sits there, they die.'

'Oh,' he said. Then after a second's thought, he added, 'So I must be Sir Galahad, mustn't I? What do you want me to do?'

'Find us a miracle, I suppose,' I said.

'Look for the Holy Grail, of course,' shouted Jenny, from her branch. 'That's what he does in the story.'

'OK,' said Gavin. 'What's a holy grail?' He was always asking questions, but I suppose that was how he came to be so clever.

'We don't know,' I told him. 'Mr Milner hasn't explained that bit yet. All I know is that it's meant to be magic.'

'It's bound to be something religious,' said Lynn helpfully. 'I bet your dad could tell us all about it.'

But the others were getting fidgety now. 'I can't see how all this is going to save the pond,' complained Perry. 'We're just wasting time if you ask me. Can't we do something useful?'

'What about the petition?' said Tracey. 'We haven't signed that yet.'

'That's true,' I said. 'I'll get some of the proper forms off the Badger Man tonight. Any other ideas?'

Everyone shrugged. Then Gary One said, 'Why don't we have a demo? We could all come and sit here and refuse to move. The workmen couldn't chop the trees down if we were in the way.'

'We could make a load of posters as well,' said Gary Two. '"Protect Our Pond." "Hands Off Our Trees." All that sort of stuff.'

'Yeah,' said Gary Three. 'And if anyone tries to shift us, we can scrag them with our banners.'

They were looking more cheerful now, at the thought of a decent protest, and I could see they were spoiling for a fight. But I was a bit worried. I had a feeling that a general punch-up still wasn't the best way to beat the builders. 'Look,' I said. 'I think we've got to try peaceful methods first. After all, it's not really the builders' fault, is it? It's the people who make the plans who have to be stopped.'

'Mmm,' agreed Perry reluctantly. 'But who are they?'

'Horrible little men with computers,' said Lynn. 'They sit in offices all day and pretend to be God. That's what my mum says.'

'That's right,' said Tracey. 'And I bet the person who decided to smash up our pond doesn't even know what a tree looks like. I bet he's never even been here.'

This comment was greeted by a chorus of cheers and stamping feet, so I broke in quickly, before the discussion turned too bloodthirsty. 'Well, let's try the petition first. And if that doesn't work, we'll have the demo instead. We'll go round the whole school, and you can all help to collect signatures.' But although they all nodded, it was obvious they wanted to do something more dramatic.

'You don't hear of knights in armour going round with soppy bits of paper, do you?' grumbled Gary One. 'I mean, it would have been a fat lot of good giving a stupid list of names to a dragon, wouldn't it?

"We the undersigned hereby demand that you stop eating people at once. Thank you." '

'He'd have just burnt the paper and eaten the lot of them,' said Gary Two.

'Yeah,' said Gary Three. 'We want a fight, don't we, boys?'

'So do we,' added Tracey and Lynn. 'We're knights too, don't forget.'

'OK,' I shouted above all the noise. 'But we'll have to practise first, so we'd better have our tournament, hadn't we? How about tomorrow, straight after school?'

'And about time too,' said Gary Two. 'I thought that was the whole point of this King Arthur game.'

'But what are we using for weapons?' asked Lynn. 'We can't actually kill each other, can we?'

'Course not, stupid,' said Alan. 'It's a conker fight. We've collected hundreds, haven't we, Perry?' Then, seeing the expression on Lynn's face, he offered to lend her a few of his spares.

'Right then,' I said. 'That's settled. All bring your best specimens and we'll have a knockout contest to see who's the bravest knight in the land.'

The daylight was just beginning to fade, and everyone suddenly realised how late it was getting. The others rushed off in various directions, to get home before trouble started, and Jenny jumped down out of the tree to help push me up the slope.

'You didn't say much,' I commented as we crunched over the gravel.

'There wasn't much to say,' she said. 'I don't really see what anyone can do. It's rotten. Specially when the pond's looking so nice. My two aunties are going to be dead upset.'

We rattled along without speaking for a bit. Lanky was staggering ahead with two school bags on his back, and his little brother was hanging on to the handles of my chair. I could hear panting noises in my ear, and I guessed that Gavin was having to run to keep up with us. 'Come on, Galahad,' I said. 'You're supposed to be the most perfect knight of all.'

'You're supposed to find the Holy Grail,' Jenny put in. 'That's what we really need. A proper miracle. A bit of real magic.'

Gavin didn't answer straight away. He was too breathless. Eventually, when we stopped outside the rectory, he managed, 'All right. I'll try. I'll look everywhere.' Which at least made the rest of us smile.

I waved my friends off, then waited for someone to help me up the ramp, but no one came so I steered myself round to the side door instead. I thumped on the glass, and Mum's face appeared behind the panel looking all wobbly and distorted like a forlorn monster.

She opened the door, and she was back to normal again. 'Good gracious,' she said with a gasp. 'Is that the time? I had no idea. We've been so busy putting the world to rights.'

In the kitchen, I found the Badger Man sitting at the table with his chin in his hands. 'Hello, lad,' he said. 'Had a good day?'

I didn't bother to go into details about school. I just went straight to the point. 'Have you got some more of your petition leaflets? We want to take them all round the school tomorrow. It's urgent, see. The workmen have come and painted rings on the trees.'

The Badger Man gazed at me glumly, and I could tell from his eyes he was beginning to give up hope. 'Thanks, lad,' he said in a flat voice. 'It's very good of you to bother. And thank all your friends as well. But I'm afraid it's too late for petitions now. The plans have been passed, and the builders start moving in at the weekend. There doesn't seem to be any way to stop them.'

I made some protesting noises, but he was already standing up ready to leave. 'Everything's signed and sealed,' he went on as he fastened his jacket. 'I've been saying to your mother, no one seems to care about trees and grass any more. It's all bricks and concrete these days.'

He pulled on his big cycling gloves and I wheeled across to the door to bar his way. 'But there must be something we can do,' I cried. 'We can't give up yet. Who's in charge? Isn't there someone we could talk to about it?'

He pulled a defeated face. 'Some rich chap called Doctor Derek More. He's the one with the cash. But he's a city type. Not interested in nature. He thinks he's doing the village a favour, building a luxury estate on derelict land.' He put one gloved hand on each of my shoulders and looked at me apologetically. 'Believe me, lad, I've tried everything. But the trouble is, we haven't really got a strong enough argument. The site just isn't important, as far as the planners are concerned.'

'But what about the trees?' I said. 'Surely they're important.'

He shrugged helplessly. 'I think so. You think so. The animals that live in them think so. But Doctor More doesn't agree. He says he's going to plant some nice new ornamental trees as soon as the site's been drained and cleared. But the old ones are too big and they're in the way.'

I couldn't accept it. 'But that's not right,' I said. 'New ones won't be any use. Trees take hundreds of years to grow. We want the chestnuts. And Arthur's Oak.' The thought of chain saws slicing through the great tree was almost too much to bear. It would be like losing a friend.

'I know,' said the Badger Man with a deep sigh. 'I want to save Arthur's Oak as much as you do. It's stood there for so long, and now some mindless vandal with a cheque book wants to destroy it. It breaks my heart. But unless we can come up with a miracle, we're helpless.'

He was squeezing past me to reach the door, but I caught at his sleeve. 'What about the Questing Beast?' I pleaded. 'I mean, the endangered species. Surely there's a chance. Isn't there?'

'Perhaps,' he said. 'I don't know. Like I say. It's going to take a miracle.' His whole body sagged as he spoke, and this time I pulled the chair back to let him escape.

I felt my mother move across the kitchen to stand behind me, and I looked up into her face as the door closed. 'Poor man,' she said. 'He came round to tell me his troubles, but I don't think I helped very much. He really cares about this village, but what can ordinary people do? Plans are made, papers are signed, and that's that. Sometimes you can hold things

86

up for a few months, but in the end it's usually a losing battle.'

My mum doesn't normally look on the gloomy side, and I was really surprised to hear her talk like that. But it made me feel all the more determined. 'Not this time,' I told her. 'Just for once we're going to win. You'll see.' And I helped her wash up the two cups that stood on the draining board, to show her how positive I felt.

Inside, of course, I wasn't quite so sure. I had the fighting spirit all right, but the method of attack was still a complete mystery. I sniffed at the air, but there were no cooking smells yet. Meals were often late in our house, because people were always dropping in unexpectedly to talk about their worries or arrange their weddings. Often, we would end up eating fish and chips at bedtime.

'Where's Dad?' I asked. 'I've got a question for him, from school. No one else seems to know the answer.'

'In the church, I think,' said Mum. 'Getting himself organised for All Hallows Day. Tell him dinner should be ready in half an hour, if you're going that way.'

And I left her rummaging through a stack of plastic bags in the freezer, while I bowled away down the garden path to the gap in our hedge. This led straight to the church porch, and although the wooden doors were a bit stiff, I could usually open them if I reversed the chair and rammed my way in backwards.

Once inside the church, the air felt chilly, but my wheels glided smoothly over the old flagstones and I zoomed down the aisle towards the altar. I could hear rustling sounds behind it, and I guessed that Dad must be sorting out the communion things. He heard me approaching, and stood up.

'Hello, son,' he said. 'Dinner ready?' He sounded hopeful, but he wasn't surprised when I delivered Mum's message. 'Such is life,' he said. 'They also serve who only stand and wait.' Then he ducked down to carry on with his unpacking.

I watched his hand reach up and plonk a large silver cup on top of the altar cloth. A dead leaf dislodged itself from a drooping flower display, and fell into the gleaming bowl.

'Dad,' I said. 'What's a holy grail? Mr Milner's getting to the end of the King Arthur story, so I was wondering.'

His face peered at me over the edge of the altar. 'The Holy Grail,' he said. 'Well, there's only one, and that's what makes it special.' He straightened up, picked the dead leaf out of the communion cup and held the shining object high to catch the last pale glimmerings of light from the windows.

'When Jesus met with his disciples for their last meal together on earth, he poured red wine into a chalice like this. Then he passed it round for everyone to share, and as they drank he told them that the wine was to remind them of his own blood.'

His voice was quiet, but it seemed to echo round the hollow building, and the top part of my spine quivered. I had heard the story of the Last Supper thousands of times, but it always gave me the shivers.

'That chalice,' my father concluded, 'was the Holy Grail.'

'Oh,' I said. 'So what happened to it after the supper ended?'

'No one knows,' Dad said. 'There are plenty of legends, of course. Some say it was brought to England by one of the first Christians, but there's never been any real proof.'

'And is it really magic?' I couldn't resist asking.

Dad laughed. 'Why not?' he said. 'We all need a little magic in our lives now and then.' He put the silver cup back in its place and stroked it fondly. 'Not that you'll find any in this poor old thing.'

It looked all right to me, not even dented. But Dad noticed my raised eyebrows and smiled. 'This is just a factory copy, I'm afraid. Quite nice, but not hand-made or anything. The original was stolen many years ago during the First World War and it's never been seen since. It was extremely beautiful, by all accounts. Solid silver and worth a small fortune. Made by a craftsman in the Middle Ages. Unfortunately, some hooligans broke in and stole it.

'The vicar who used to live here heard them, and gave chase. But although some farm hands helped catch the thieves, the chalice itself had disappeared.'

'The men must have hidden it,' I said. 'Or thrown it away. Into a haystack or something.'

'I suppose so,' agreed my father, giving the imita-tion chalice a rub with his sleeve. 'But whether they ever came back for it we'll never know. Some say they volunteered to fight in France, instead of going to prison, and were killed in the trenches. But that's probably just another of those old stories.' He glanced at his watch. 'Fifteen minutes to go,' he announced. 'That's if we don't have any more visitors. Come on, son. Let's go and warm up in the house.'

He pushed me out of the heavy doors, and let them

creak shut behind us. Before I could make any comment, he said, 'After the theft, the villagers voted to buy a cheap replacement. They didn't want to lock the doors of God's house, but they didn't want to risk losing any more valuables.'

I nodded. I could understand how the people had felt. I wouldn't have wanted to build barricades round the village pond. 'Vandals still come, but nowadays they steal our trees instead.' I said. But the idea of robbers with oak trees in their swagbags was silly enough to put us both in a good mood, and we were quite giggly by the time we got indoors.

The house smelt of beefburgers and fried onions, so as soon as we had both used the downstairs toilet, we made for the dining room. Kit was already there, sitting at the table in his track suit. His face was hot, and there were little beads of sweat at the sides of his nose.

'Been for a run,' he said. 'There's nothing like it. You've got to keep fit, you know.'

'So you keep telling us,' I said. 'Did you know they're going to chop down the trees by the pond? We've got to stop them. What can we do?' But if I was hoping for a sensible suggestion from Kit, I was wasting my breath. He was just as useless as bossy Sir Kay in the stories.

All he said was, 'Give up, kiddo. You can't argue with bulldozers. Pass the water. I'm dying of thirst.'

Dad went out to help Mum with the tray, and the food arrived. But just as we were all lifting our forks to our mouths, the doorbell rang.

'I don't believe it,' said Mum crossly. 'If it's another cat in a cardboard box, you can tell it to wait in the queue.' Then she sat glowering at Dad's plate of chips, which were turning cold and soggy while he answered the door.

It wasn't a cat. It was Jenny's two mad aunties, popping in on their way to arrange some fresh flowers in the church. We all listened as we chewed. Their sad wails trickled down the hall and drifted in through the dining room door. 'Wicked shame. Arthur's Oak. The chestnuts. The pond. Terrible. Dreadful.'

Somehow, Dad managed to pacify them with a few comforting phrases, but when he got back, Mum was fuming. 'That Doctor More has got a lot to answer for,' she grumbled. 'First he upsets the whole village with his wretched plans. Then he makes your dinner late. And now your food's gone stone cold. I'd like to give that man a piece of my mind. I really would.'

Which was funny enough to set the rest of us giggling again. All the same, I knew exactly how she felt, and that night as I lay in bed I tried to imagine what Doctor More must look like. A tall, sinister man wearing a striped suit and a spiky moustache, I decided. A man with small eyes and a thin, cruel mouth. A real arch-enemy.

'You wait,' I thought. 'I'll beat you yet. I don't know how, but you're going to lose this battle, Doctor Derek More.'

6   The Grand Tournament

It's one thing to sound brave and fearless when you're lying in bed pretending to be a hero. It's something else when you actually see a ten-ton truck driving down the road towards you. This one was large and yellow, and it definitely seemed out to get me.

I was on my way to school and just rounding the bend near the village pub when it rumbled past me for the first time. I was almost at the school gates, and had been joined by Gavin and Lanky, when it appeared for the second time. It was moving very slowly, and its front grill seemed to snarl at us like a mouthful of menacing steel teeth.

I pushed down against the rims of my wheels to speed up, but the monster crunched to a halt, and a bearded face emerged from the nearside window. 'Oi! You kids. Which way to the village pond?'

I was caught completely off my guard. Strangers rarely bother to ask me questions, because they tend to think that people in wheelchairs have paralysed brains. So this time I was feeling flattered, and immediately launched into a detailed description of the route the truck should take. 'You're nearly there. All you have to do is . . .'

Then I realized that the man wasn't listening to me

after all. He was far more interested in Lanky, which served him right. Lanky always used to panic when someone asked for directions.

'Er. Um. Let's see. If you turn round and . . . No. Wait a minute. Keep going till you get to the bend, then go left. Or is it right? No. Um . . .'

The bearded face stopped grinning. 'All right, sunshine. Forget it. I'll ask someone else.' And the machine roared back into life, before smothering us in choking exhaust fumes. As it thundered away down the road, I noticed that the back was piled high with drainpipes and concrete slabs.

'Well done, Lanky,' I said. 'At least you managed to confuse them for a bit. Not that it'll make much difference in the long run.'

The sky was very grey and overcast that morning, which suited our mood. We were all wearing our waterproofs, and little Gavin was clomping along in a pair of old wellies that had once belonged to Lanky. 'I've brought a jam jar as well,' he was telling me in his excited way. 'And I'm going to explore the pond after school.' But I was only listening with half an ear. I was far more concerned about the drizzle that had begun to soak through my trousers, than I was about first-year pond-dipping expeditions.

The drizzle had turned to proper rain by the time the bell rang, and I was glad to get indoors. It was a good job we were looking forward to our lessons that day, because there wasn't much else to be cheerful about.

'Did you bring the petitions?' Tracey asked as soon as I reached the classroom. So I had to explain everything the Badger Man had told me the night before, and was greeted by a chorus of groans and grumbles.

'Typical,' said Gary One. 'I bet if any of us dared to snap off one weedy twig, we'd be in big trouble for vandalism. But grown-ups are allowed to come and chop down the whole blinking lot if they feel like it. S'not fair.'

Mr Milner walked into the room at that point, and wanted to know the reason for all the fuss. He should have known better, because he was nearly deafened by the explosion of protests, and ended up banging on his desk for silence. 'Art,' he said wearily. 'Perhaps you would care to explain. In a normal voice, if at all possible.'

So I spoke as calmly as I could, but it was difficult not to get carried away when I was feeling so angry. '. . . So, you see,' I finished, 'it's too late. There's nothing we can do about it now. The lorries are arriving already.'

Mr Milner nodded sympathetically. 'However,' he said, 'the trees still stand, so we must not despair yet. The battle is lost, but the war has still to be won.'

'But, sir,' I said, 'we can't beat the builders, can we?' I was thinking of the cardboard shields and banners we had been making, and how useless they would be in a fight against bearded workmen with sledgehammers.

Mr Milner smiled. 'There's more than one way to cross a moat,' he said. 'Always remember, my boy, that the pen is mightier than the sword.' Which all sounded very mysterious and clever, but as far as I was concerned, made no sense at all.

In fact, the whole class seemed to be depressed and

moody after that. The room grew greyer, the rain got worse and we became more and more irritable as the morning wore on. When our outdoor break was cancelled, that was just about the last straw. We all sat round the room in dejected huddles, picking at our crisps and playing boring games like word-search and hangman.

'Let's hang Doctor More,' I said bitterly, when it was my turn to choose the clue. 'He's the one who's causing all the trouble.'

'Is he?' said Lanky, with a puzzled frown. 'And who's Doctor More when he's at home? I've never heard of him.'

'He's the man who bought the site,' I said. 'He's in charge of everything. It's all his idea.'

'Well, I wish he was coming to the tournament tonight,' said Gary Two. 'We'd soon make him change his mind, wouldn't we, boys?'

'Yeah,' said Gary Three. 'We'd scrag him.'

'I'd put a spell on him and turn him into a slimy little toad,' said Jenny. 'Serve him right, too.'

'Didn't the Badger Man have any ideas at all?' asked Lynn. 'I don't want to give up yet.'

I shook my head. 'Just the usual stuff, about needing a miracle.'

'Miracles,' grumbled Alan. 'That's all anyone ever talks about. I don't believe in miracles.'

'What about the Holy Grail, then?' asked Tracey 'Perhaps we could go and look for that.'

'No use,' I told her. 'My dad say it's only a legend. The special cup Jesus used at the Last Supper. And even if it still exists, it's hardly going to turn up in our crummy village, is it?'

'Don't see why not,' said Perry. 'It's got to turn up somewhere, so why not here?' But of course, that was only a daydream and we all knew it.

'We could look for the old communion chalice,' I suggested to cheer everyone up. 'It's not exactly magic, but it is worth a lot of money.'

No one was very impressed. We still weren't any closer to saving the pond, and our only chance seemed to be a sit-in protest at the site. The thought of waiting under Arthur's Oak for days and weeks, until the workmen went away, was daunting. And I had a nasty feeling it wasn't going to be very practical. I mean, there aren't any toilets near the pond, for a start. And how many people were likely to volunteer for the night shift, even if their mums would let them do it.

Still, it was agreed. The others mooched off to find some comics and playing cards, to help pass the rest of our wet break, and left me fiddling with the hangman paper. I had Excalibur in my pocket, so I started to doodle around with the letters of the alphabet. Anagrams. My favourite game.

'Dr More', I wrote. Then, to make it look more official, 'Dr D. More'. I was wondering whether it would be worth writing him a letter, and whether the Badger Man would deliver it for me. As I thought, I juggled with the words to see what would emerge. Drome. Dormer. Modem. Nothing quite perfect. I really wanted to use every letter in the name, and I wished I had my Scrabble pieces with me.

Then suddenly, everything clicked into place; and Excalibur flew into top gear. When I'd finished, I stared at the new arrangement in disbelief. I was remembering what Mr Milner had told us the night before. How the arrival of Galahad would bring both the Holy Grail and the final, terrible battle. The Round Table would be finished, and Arthur would be beaten by his greatest enemy. The most evil knight of all. Sir Mordred.

And there was his name, on the page before me. Dr D. More and the arch-fiend were one and the same. My mouth felt parched, but I looked round the room for someone to tell about my discovery. Lanky, Jenny, anyone. They were all burrowing in cupboards or arguing in corners. I tried to shout, but the words wouldn't come and I sat there like a demented goldfish blowing invisible bubbles. Sir Mordred. Sir Mordred.

The bell went before I got any further, and by lunch time I'd decided to keep my fears to myself. At least until after the tournament. Let the others enjoy themselves while they could. All the same, I was un-naturally quiet and moody and more than glad when afternoon lessons began.

That day, we were finishing off our King Arthur project. Mr Milner had plans to begin something new on Monday, so this was our last chance to paint our shields and banners. We were using the class powder paints, mixed to a stodgy thickness, and a set of flashy felt pens that Mr Milner had ordered specially. Gold and silver and copper, to outline our designs.

The final results looked quite professional, and we all felt rather pleased with ourselves. So we were glad to find there was enough time left for a quick drama session, acting out the best bits of the story so far.

Mr Milner had copied some of main speeches on to sheets of paper and rolled them to look like scrolls. He gave me one of these, and asked me to read the part where King Arthur makes his royal pledge to the knights. Before I started, he placed a thin golden crown of painted card on my head. 'Just a simple circlet,' he explained. 'For everyday use on the battlefield.'

Lanky and the others sat in a circle on the floor with their shields propped up in front of them, while I uncurled my script and read out, 'If I am indeed King, I hereby pledge myself to the service of God and of my people. To the rightings of wrongs, to the driving out of evil, and to the bringing of peace and plenty to my land.'

As soon as I stopped, everyone began cheering wildly and shaking their banners, which took me completely by surprise. I had been feeling so defeated and despondent, but now I was King Arthur again. Powerful and important. And also ashamed of my own cowardice. A true king would never give up trying, however hopeless things might seem. He would keep on fighting, right to the very end, Sir Mordred or no Sir Mordred. And so would I.

'Very good, Art,' said Mr Milner. His voice sounded strange, as though his throat was blocked, and he had to cough before he could go on. 'Now, try this short piece, before we dramatize a few of the adventures.'

This time, it was Arthur's first speech to the new knights of the Round Table. The list of rules. Pretty stirring stuff. 'I lay upon you the Order of Chivalry. Do not ever depart from the High Virtues of this realm. Do no cruel or wicked thing. Fly from untruthfulness and dishonest dealing. Give mercy to those who seek it. Give all help in your power, and never fight in any quarrel that is not just or righteous.'

Again, I was greeted by enthusiastic applause, and I sat there glowing while the others went off to perform various quests in different corners of the classroom. It was great fun. Jenny went round being Morgana, and cackling in everyone's ears, while I took over as cheerleader, encouraging all the good knights to win.

With a few minutes left before home time, Mr Milner called us all together again, and we grouped round him still carrying our shields and banners. I felt full of confidence. I knew my crown was only made of cardboard, but that didn't matter. I felt more like King Arthur than ever before. It was as though I could face any enemy, win any battle, and no one could stand against me.

I remembered Arthur's Oak and the village pond, and it seemed to me that I could roll the bulldozers away single-handed if I wanted. I was so strong. A real leader.

Some of the others sounded out of breath, and I knew they had been living their parts too. Even Lanky looked bright-eyed and excited. 'How does the story end, sir?' he asked. 'Is there really a big battle? Does Arthur ever find the Holy Grail?'

'Listen,' said Mr Milner with a shake of his bony finger. 'And I'll tell you.'

But in a way I wished he hadn't. I would much rather not have known.

He didn't bother with the book at all that day. He just leaned back against the window and talked. But as his voice drew the pictures, his face grew more and more serious and I felt my whole body shrink into my chair. The fun and laughter of the drama lesson was nothing but a memory now, and I seemed to have lost my way inside one of those nightmares where the world goes crazy. Why did the end of the story have to be so awful? Why didn't King Arthur tell his knights to forget about the Holy Grail?

But he let them go, even though he knew most of them would never return. A few died on the way, and many were lost forever. Even Sir Galahad, who actually managed to find the chalice, died soon after he had seen it. And then everything else started to go wrong as well.

Morgana's power spread like a poisonous disease, making the other knights forget their Order of Chivalry. Lancelot, Arthur's most faithful friend, was driven out of the kingdom as a traitor and chased into France. When he fought back, he accidentally killed Gawain, and although he tried to make his peace with the king, he was sent into exile. So Arthur was left with hardly any true friends. Guinevere ran away from Camelot, and the wicked knight, Sir Mordred, spread evil rumours and stirred up arguments all the time.

In the end, there was a final great battle between the knights who were left, and nearly everyone died of their wounds. Arthur found himself facing Mordred alone, and the two mortal enemies vowed to fight each other to the death. Arthur managed to beat Mordred, but lay dying himself, and there was just Sir Bedivere alive to care for him.

He told his only friend to throw Excalibur back into the lake, but at first Sir Bedivere refused. It seemed such a dreadful thing to do. When at last he did as he was asked, he saw a woman's arm reach up out of the water to receive the magic sword. Then Excalibur disappeared forever.

I was almost in tears at that point. It all seemed such a waste. All that courage and goodness gone for nothing. The classroom around me was still and silent. No one had the heart to cough or fidget. We were all watching Mr Milner's face, and hoping there would be something more to come. Something positive.

We should have known he wouldn't disappoint us. Perhaps we did. Anyway, he gave himself a little shake, as if waking from a bad dream, and said, 'Then, from out of the swirling mist, there floated a black barge, and inside it three figures, like ravens of darkness. The ladies of the lake. And one of them was Morgana, who had finally given up her evil ways.

'Sir Bedivere helped them place the dying king inside the barge, and they all sailed away, never to be seen again.'

We all brightened up. 'So did King Arthur die?' I asked. 'Was that really the end? Or did he get better?'

'No one knows,' said Mr Milner. 'Some say it was all a legend, but others tell how Arthur and his knights were taken to a secret cave, where they still lie sleeping.'

He moved over to his desk, picked up his book, and flipped it open at the last page. 'Here are Arthur's final words to Bedivere, before the funeral barge disappeared,' he said. And he read out the king's promise. '"Be you sure that I will come again, when my land has need of me, and my realm shall rise once more out of the darkness. But if you never hear of me more, pray for my soul."'

'So Arthur could come back, then. If he was really needed by someone.' It was Jenny who spoke, and I looked at her in surprise. I hadn't expected her to take any of this so seriously.

'Perhaps,' answered Mr Milner, laying the book to one side.

'But how could he? Wouldn't he need some sort of disguise?' She was clearly determined not to let the matter drop, and I waited tensely for Mr Milner to speak.

All he said was, 'Perhaps. Perhaps not. That, my dear, is something we shall never know.'

I could see from her face that Jenny would have liked to say more, but the bell cut her short. Mr Milner dismissed us, and we all made a rush to clear our desks and grab our shields and banners.

'Can I keep my crown, sir?' I asked hopefully. He didn't reply. He just nodded. But as I turned away, I was sure he murmured something. Either that, or the words crept into my brain by themselves.

'Do not despair. Remember. The pen is mightier than the sword.'

I glanced back over my shoulder, but he was busy with our maths books and didn't appear to notice me.

'Come on, Art,' said Lanky. 'Let's get down to the pond before the rain starts again. We've got to have our tournament before the builders dig everything up.'

We all got away from school as fast as we could. No one bothered to hang around eating sweets or gossiping in the cloakrooms. We were all too horribly aware that this was probably our last meeting before the village pond and Arthur's Oak disappeared forever.

By the time I had covered the distance in my chair,

most of the others were already yelling battle cries, or testing out their prize conkers. Lanky helped to steer me past the mountain of drainpipes and concrete blocks the lorry had dumped on the grass that morning, and I started to call for order.

'We'll have two people at a time,' I announced, 'and I'll be the umpire. We'll keep going till we have one winner, and he'll be the champion.'

'Who says it's going to be a boy?' Tracey objected. 'My conker's just as good as anyone else's. So there.'

'Rubbish,' jeered Gary One. 'Anyway, it's not the conker that counts. It's the person using it.'

'You need decent muscles for this game,' agreed Gary Two. 'You girls don't stand a chance.'

'Yeah,' said Gary Three. 'I don't know why you lot bothered to come. We'll scrag you. Easy.'

'Oh no you won't,' shrieked Lynn. 'We'll show them, won't we, Tracey?'

Things were getting out of hand already, so I pulled a piece of paper out of my bag and reached for Excalibur. Perhaps if I made a start on the score sheet, the others would remember what we were supposed to be doing. I noticed I was holding the leftover hangman game, with 'Dr D. More' and 'Mordred' still written on it, and that made me more impatient than ever.

'Shut up,' I bellowed. 'We're wasting time. The whole point of this tournament is to get ourselves ready for the battle with the builders. Like proper knights. So let's get going.' I wrote down two names, and added, 'Galahad and Percival are first. Where are they?'

Perry performed a quick fanfare, and leapt out from

under the trees with his shield in one hand and his conker in the other. 'Ta da,' he cried. 'Come on, Gavin. Do your worst.'

There was no answer. Lanky's little brother was far too interested in the mud round the edge of the water, to come when he was called. He was making the most of his wellingtons, and sploshing out as far as he dared towards the middle of the pond.

'Hurry up, Gavin,' I nagged. 'We need you for the first round.'

'Don't want to,' he yelled back. 'I'm Sir Galahad. I'm looking for the Holy Grail.'

'Oh, leave him,' said Lanky irritably. 'There's no point arguing with him. He never listens.'

'All right,' I said, trying to sound calm. 'Agravaine. Let's have you instead.'

Alan and Perry stood facing each other, and waited for me to give the signal while the others grouped round to cheer them on. Then they put their shields on the grass, and prepared to make their first strike. Just as Alan was about to swing his conker, there came a loud squeal from the direction of the water.

'I've found it. I've found it. Look everybody. It's the Holy Grail.'

Alan swore, and his conker missed its target. 'You stupid idiot,' he roared. 'You've made me lose my turn.'

We all looked at Gavin, who was dancing around joyfully, and splashing muddy water everywhere. In his hands he held a brown, slimy object which dripped green blobs on to his sleeves.

'Put it down, Gav,' grumbled Lanky. 'It's only an old tin can. Leave it alone before you . . .' But he was too late. His little brother had skidded on a loose stone, lost his balance and fallen straight into the mud. 'Oh no,' groaned Lanky. 'I'll get the blame for that. I'm supposed to be looking after him.'

'One down,' called a voice, and someone began to laugh.

'What's so funny?' Lanky demanded. 'Don't make fun of my brother, Gary, or I'll punch you on the nose.'

'I wasn't laughing,' said Gary One. 'Don't look at me.'

'Well someone did.' Lanky stamped down the slope to drag his brother away from the water, and the teasing laughter rang out again. He swung round fiercely, and I could see his hands were trembling. 'OK, I definitely heard you that time.' He tried to run back towards the three Garys, but the grass was so slippery from the day's drizzle that he slid backwards clumsily, whirling his arms to keep himself from falling.

At the same moment, Gary One let out a yelp of pain. He was clutching the side of his head. 'You threw a stone at me,' he shouted. 'That's dangerous, Lanky. You could have knocked my eye out.'

Lanky was staggering up the slope again, and I could see that he was ready for a fight. He didn't lose his temper very often, but the sight of Gavin's filthy clothes must have really rattled him. 'I haven't touched you,' he said. 'You started it. Laughing at me and Gav.'

The next minute, Gary and Lanky were rolling about in the grass, and squashing the shields that Alan and Perry had left there. 'Oi,' they complained.

'Get up. Gerroff our shields.' Then they piled on top of the other two, while I wheeled over to try to stop them.

'Gawain. Lancelot. Pack it in,' I yelled. 'This is supposed to be a tournament, not a wrestling match. Your mums'll go mad when you get home.'

The girls were gathering round now for a better view, and Gavin came squelching up to stand beside them. 'I'm cold,' he whimpered. 'I wanna go home.'

Somehow, Lanky managed to extricate himself from the tangle of bodies just as the remaining two Garys charged in to join the scrum. He crawled out from under their legs, and made a feeble attempt to scrape the mud off his lenses with a wet finger. 'All right,' he muttered to Gavin. 'I'll take you home. But don't you dare blame this lot on me.' He snatched at his brother's sleeve and hauled him away through the trees.

'Cowardy cowardy custard,' sneered Gary Two, who had just straightened up to jump on Alan's conker.

'He's not a coward,' said Lynn. 'He's only looking after his little brother, that's all.'

'Oh yeah?' said Gary Three.

'Yeah,' said Tracey. 'So make something out of that if you can.'

But the others didn't say anything. Gary One was peeling dead leaves off his sweater, and making sniffling noises in the back of his nose, while Alan and Perry tried to repair their battered shields.

'You boys messed up everything,' complained Lynn. 'We were really looking forward to a proper conker fight, weren't we, Tracey?'

'Well, it wasn't our fault,' began Alan. 'We were OK until . . .' But then all hell let loose again. Everyone was shouting at everyone else and jumping about in agony.

'You hit me.'

'No I didn't.'

'Yes you did.'

'Gerroff . . . Stoppit . . . Wait till I get you. . . .'

And I sat there in dismay, watching my Round Table gang do their best to scrag each other. Acorns and conkers were whizzing in all directions, and it was impossible to tell who was firing what, or when. 'Stop,' I cried at the top of my voice. 'Please. This isn't right at all.'

But no one was listening, and I think they would probably have carried on all night if the rain hadn't suddenly started. It was only a few drops at first, but enough to make everyone remember where they were. Alan and Perry sprinted off to collect what was left of their shields, and the girls balanced their own banners over their hair.

'That was a great fight, fellas,' said Gary Three. 'Thanks. See you, Art.' And he was away up the slope.

'Hey, wait,' I said. 'You can't go yet. . . .' It was no use. They were all leaving, pulling up their coat collars, and holding up their shields to keep off the worst of the rain. 'No.' I was frantic now. 'Please. Don't you see? That was only a practice. We've got to put up a proper fight now. Stay here and stop the builders, before it's too late. Come back. I thought you all wanted to help.'

Gary Three looked back at me over his shoulder.

'Not in the rain,' he said. 'My mum goes barmy if I get my feet wet. She scrags me.'

And soon they had all gone, chasing up the bank and along the path towards the village centre. I pressed down on my wheels to follow them, but the slope was against me so the best I could do was head for Arthur's Oak and shelter under the branches. The rain was getting through, but at least there were enough leaves left to stop me getting soaked.

I sat there, staring at the grey pond while my face grew wet and cold. Everything was over. Finished. And I was a failure. I stuffed my sheet of soggy paper back in my pocket and jammed the top on my pen. Poor old Excalibur. A drop of salt water dripped off the end of my nose, and I tried to wipe my face with a damp sleeve.

'Oi. Don't start crying.' The voice startled me, and I span round to see who was there. 'I'm up here, dozy. You didn't think I'd go off and leave you like the rest of them, did you?'

Gazing down at me from the tree was Jenny's face. She swung herself sideways and landed beside me in a flurry of snapped twigs. 'That was brilliant,' she said with a giggle. 'Really funny. You should have seen yourselves.'

'Morgana,' I groaned. 'I might have known. I bet it was you who laughed at Lanky.'

'Yep,' she said proudly. 'And it was me who whizzed acorns at everyone. Did you hear them shout? Good, wasn't it? And no one guessed it was me. Just like in the story.'

'Yes.' I nodded gloomily. 'Just like in the story.

Except there isn't a Sir Bedivere to throw Excalibur in the lake for me.'

'Don't talk daft,' she said. 'You can't throw a perfectly good pen away. In any case, I keep telling you, it's only a game. You shouldn't take it all so seriously.'

'I can't help it,' I said. 'Everything's gone wrong, hasn't it? We'll never have another Round Table meeting, because there won't even be anywhere to meet.'

'Mmm,' she said. Then she gave my arm a nudge. 'Cheer up, Adam. We aren't beaten yet. There must be a way out.'

I shook my head. 'No,' I said. 'It's hopeless.'

But she had started giggling again. 'I suppose you're expecting my two aunties to come sailing across the pond in a big black boat, to carry you away. You really are daft, you know. After all . . .' Here she stood up triumphantly, and waved her arms in the air, 'you can't give up yet. You haven't had your fight with Sir Mordred, have you? So there must be more to come.'

I was about to answer her, when the sound of someone running towards us broke my concentration. Heavy feet were slapping across the grass, and I could hear the sounds of painful breathing. We both turned our heads to see who it could be, and saw a small man with a red nose and dripping hair. He dived under the tree, and stood there shivering. Then I coughed, and he realised he was not alone.

'S'cuse me,' he said, blowing his nose violently into an enormus blue handkerchief. 'Is there room for one more?'

'Of course,' said Jenny, budging up to make room for him on the seat. 'Wet, isn't it?'

'Certainly is,' said the man. 'I parked my car at the other end of the village. I didn't realize the pond would be this far. And then the rain started. Aaaa-choo!' He sneezed so hard his whole body rocked, and he smiled at us apologetically over the top of his hanky. 'Sorry. S'cuse me. I'm not used to weather. I'm usually indoors all day. When I'm not in the car.'

We nodded and tried to look friendly. He seemed very nervous and miserable, sitting there in his wet clothes. We both knew all the rules about not talking to strangers, but this little man didn't look strong enough to kidnap two children and a wheelchair.

'Want a fizzy scruncher?' I suggested. 'It'll help pass the time till the rain stops.'

'Love it,' said the man. He picked the fluff off a scruncher and popped it in his mouth. Then he took a thin black pen from his pocket, and gave his nose a final wipe on the enormous handkerchief.

In one corner of the crumpled cloth, clearly embroidered in dark blue thread, was a squiggly initial. The letter D.

7   Mordred

'Who goes first?' I asked, straightening out the crumpled piece of paper on my lap.

'You can,' said the man. 'But you'll have to remind me of the rules. I haven't played Hangman for years.'

So I drew a row of blanks, in two groups. Four, then six. 'This is a character from a book,' I said. 'And you're sitting under his tree. That's a clue.'

'Now you have to guess the missing letters,' explained Jenny. 'I'll help you if you like.' So she suggested an 'L', which was wrong, and I began to draw the little hangman picture. Just the base to start with, but it soon grew. Between them, they seemed to pick on every letter in the alphabet, except the ones they needed.

At last, the man guessed an 'I' and watched as I filled a space in the first word, but he was still stuck. 'Tiny Tim?' he muttered. 'No. That doesn't fit. Bill Somebody? Miss Muffett? No. Oh dear.' Then he made a guess at 'E', which was sensible but useless.

'You're dead, I'm afraid,' I announced, drawing the last part of the design so that a body hung from the gallows.

'Who was it, then?' asked Jenny. I couldn't really believe she didn't know, but I filled in the remaining letters anyway.

'King Arthur,' cried the man. 'I should have realised. I used to love those stories when I was your age.'

'Adam likes them too,' said Jenny. 'That's why he's wearing his crown.'

I had forgotten all about it, and I reached up to feel the circle of card. It was rather limp from the rain, but still in place, like a party hat at bedtime. The man laughed.

'I see,' he said. 'And do you mean to tell me this is the famous oak tree? I've heard so much about it.'

'That's right,' I said, passing him the sheet of paper. 'But it won't be here for much longer. It's going to be chopped down, you know. All the trees are. And the pond's going to be drained. It's terrible.'

The man had his head on one side like an inquisitive sparrow, and he was listening carefully to everything I said. 'Go on,' he urged me. 'This seems to be something you really care about.'

'Oh, it is,' I agreed. 'Because of the Badger Man, you see. He told me all about it. The trees are homes for hundreds of animals. Birds and beetles and squirrels. And loads of things live in the pond. But they'll all die once the builders start, because there's nowhere else for them to go. We wanted to help, but it's too late now. Look.' I pointed at the white execution lines round the trees, and the stack of drainpipes waiting beside the road. 'The Badger Man says we'll need a miracle now. If only we could find something rare, like an otter or a beaver, that might do the trick.'

I was beginning to feel all choked up again. 'It's all that Doctor More's fault,' I finished. 'He's the one who could change things. But he's never even been here, so how can he understand?'

The man was studying the row of lines he had drawn on the piece of paper and he didn't answer, so I started to make wild guesses. 'S,' I said. 'K? R? Y? U?' There were only seven spaces altogether, so the game should have been easy for me, but I suppose I wasn't concentrating properly. Even when I had managed an E and an A, the pattern still didn't give me any clues.

Before long, the man was ready to fill in the last part of the hanging body. 'Go on,' he said encouragingly. 'One more try.'

'It's stopped raining,' cried Jenny. 'Look.'

And sure enough, the sky had begun to clear, although it was already becoming hazy with evening. 'Good,' said the man, putting his pen back in his top pocket and passing the game across to me. 'Now I can have a look round this place. I didn't want to drive all the way here from London for nothing.'

'Well, here comes the best person to show you,' I said. The Badger Man had just skidded up to us on his bike.

He jumped off sideways, and leaned the handlebars against the oak tree. 'Your mum was worried about you,' he said. 'Asked me to come and look for you. Everything all right?'

'Yes, thanks,' I told him. 'We were just sheltering from the rain, that's all. It came down in buckets.'

'That's what I thought,' he said. 'D'you want a push up the slope?'

'In a minute. Yes, please. We were just going to have a last look round the pond.' I waved a hand at the little man, who had stepped out from under the tree and was now gazing up at its network of crooked fingers. 'He's driven here specially,' I explained. 'He wants to see Arthur's Oak and everything.'

'Well, it's a good job you came when you did,' the Badger Man told him. 'There wouldn't have been anything left to see if you'd waited much longer.'

'So I'm told,' murmured the little man. Then he stretched out his hand. 'You must be the Badger Man,' he said. 'Very pleased to meet you. And I'm Dr Derek More. I think perhaps you've heard of me.'

For a full minute, or so it seemed, we all stood with our mouths open. My brain was racing. I was frantically trying to remember all the things I had said, and my ears were burning despite the cold. Had I been very insulting? How was I to know I had been criticising the enemy himself? I mean, this friendly little person with the running nose just didn't look like an evil villain with a chainsaw.

'I'm sorry,' I began. 'I didn't mean . . .'

'Think nothing of it,' he said. 'You weren't to know. I should have introduced myself before.'

'But what brought you here?' asked the Badger Man. His voice was perfectly polite, but there was no warmth in it although he stepped forward to shake the extended hand.

'Ah, well,' said Doctor More. 'It was this letter. It arrived in the post this morning, and I felt I simply couldn't ignore it.' Out from his inside pocket, he drew a large brown envelope. And from that he took a folded wodge of familiar lined paper. School paper.

Wheeling myself closer, I leaned over for a better look, and gasped at what I saw. 'But that's mine,' I said. 'It's my story. The one I wrote for Mr Milner, about the pond and the trees. It's the best thing I've ever done, because I was using Excalibur. But how on earth . . .?'

'I think your teacher must have sent it to me,' said Doctor More. 'And I must say, I'm extremely glad he did. Extremely glad.' He took a few steps towards the pond, and swung round to take in the full view. 'So this is it,' he said. 'And you say this should be made into a nature reserve.'

'Yes,' I said hopefully. 'I know it doesn't look very exciting yet, but . . .'

The little man wasn't listening. He was prodding at something with his foot. It was the old tin can Gavin had pulled out of the pond, and which now lay on its side in the mud. 'Looks to me as though someone's been using this place as a rubbish tip,' he said. 'That's what I was told, you see. Just an area of waste land, going to rack and ruin.'

He stooped down, then immediately sprang backwards with a cry of horror. 'It moved,' he squeaked. 'That lump of mud definitely moved. And I'll swear it looked at me.'

His finger shook as he indicated the spot, and the Badger Man hurried over to investigate. 'It's a toad,' he laughed. 'Must have been disturbed somehow. It ought to be hibernating at the moment, but the weather's been so mild I suppose it was only half asleep.'

He lifted up the warty creature, and held it gently in his palms. 'It's a beauty, Adam,' he said. 'Do you notice the markings on its back?'

'Yes,' I said. 'It's a bit like the one you showed me

115

in your book. The one with the weird name. The something-or-other toad. I can't quite remember it.'

The Badger Man straightened his back and peered at the animal, which sat like a soft stone in his hand. 'My God,' he cried. 'I do believe you're right. Here, hold this for a minute, would you?' And he thrust the toad into Doctor More's hand before the astonished man could protest. Then he charged across to his bike and dragged his identification book out of the saddle bag.

He was back in seconds, with his finger on the vital illustration. 'Natterjack toad,' he cried breathlessly. 'Endangered species. I can't believe it. It's a miracle. An absolute miracle.'

'Gavin said this was the Holy Grail,' giggled Jenny, holding up the old tin. 'And it's certainly done the trick, so perhaps he was right after all.'

'That's a funny-looking tin can,' I said, studying it for the first time. 'It's too big, for a start. And it's got lumps and bulges all over it.'

'Just mud, I expect,' said Jenny, but she bent down to dunk it in the water. She scraped off several layers of gunge with a piece of twig, and then handed the wet object to me. 'What do you make of it?' she asked.

I grinned, 'Well,' I said. 'It's either a toad's hibernation hole. Or a metal wine glass. Or it's . . .' But there I paused. I didn't need any more guesses. I knew exactly what I was holding, because I had seen a perfect copy only the day before, when I went to talk with my father in the church.

'The Holy Grail,' I whispered to myself. Then out loud, I said, 'It's the village communion chalice. The real one. It's been missing since the First World War, and now Sir Galahad has found it for us.'

Back at the rectory, we all gathered in the kitchen for a warming mug of soup. All of us, that is, except for the toad, which the Badger Man had photographed, then placed carefully back in the mud. Mum was cleaning the chalice on the draining board, attacking it with soap, water and a soft nail brush.

'Your father will be thrilled,' she said. 'He'll be able to use this on All Hallows' Day. In fact, the whole village is going to be delighted.'

'Perhaps,' said Doctor More, 'I can give them something else to celebrate at the same time.'

I bit my lip, too nervous to ask him what he meant. He took a deep gulp of soup, which left him with a red moustache under his sore nose. Then he blew noisily into his handkerchief and sighed. 'I'm so glad I came here today,' he said. 'So glad. I read your story, Adam, and it made me see everything in a different light. Oh dear. When I think of all the harm I might have done.'

'Do you mean you've changed the plans?' cried Jenny. 'Oh, Doctor More. You're lovely. I knew you would.' And she actually kissed him, which isn't like Jenny at all.

The little man gave an embarrassed wriggle and straightened his tie. 'It's the least I could do,' he said. 'Has anyone got a piece of paper?'

'I have,' I said. 'Here.' I pushed the hangman sheet towards him, and noticed that the unfinished game was still there, waiting for the last letters to be filled in. Now, glancing at the pattern of lines, the answer came to me with no effort at all. 'Camelot,' I shouted. 'The missing word was Camelot.'

'Quite right,' said Doctor More. 'Well done. Looks as though I lost that game as well.' He produced his pen, and it was then that I realized he was left handed.

'Wait a minute,' I said. 'Borrow my pen. It's really good. You'll like it.' And I watched as he moved Excalibur over the page, making a quick sketch of the pond and its adjoining stretch of land.

'You see,' he told us, 'it's quite simple. We keep all this area as a nature reserve. Employ a warden to keep it tidy and organise a nature trail round the pond. Then the houses can be a bit further down the road, here. It means I'll have to lose a few buildings, of course, but that won't matter because the rest will have doubled their value anyway. As you say, my boy, people would much rather live somewhere beautiful, than find themselves surrounded by concrete.'

The Badger Man moved across to admire the new scheme. 'Marvellous,' he said. 'There's a badger sett a little further up the road in this direction, and Jenny's aunties have a decent warren on their land. So there's plenty to see.' He showed Doctor More where Aunt Ava and Aunt Lonnie lived, at Morgan's Folly, and I winked at Jenny. The two old ladies would be so relieved to hear the news, and I knew she must be dying to tell them.

My mother had phoned Jenny's family to let them know where she was, and when her father arrived to collect her, she was out of the door in a flash. 'She's not Morgana this evening,' I thought. 'Just good old Jenny. Back to normal.'

Meanwhile, the Badger Man and the Doctor had

been discussing their ideas, and I could see that the little man was fascinated. He kept asking more and more questions about the local animals, and with every answer his nose seemed to grow shinier. 'You know,' he said when the Badger Man paused for breath, 'you're just the sort of person I need for my Warden. Would you be at all interested in the job? I'd pay you well. Perhaps I could arrange to have a small bungalow built for you, as near as possible to the nature reserve. What do you say?'

What could he say? What could any of us say, come to that? Even my dad was speechless when he came in, and that's a pretty rare thing for a rector, I can tell you.

Only Kit had a comment to make, but just for once he was impressed too. 'Well, I've got to hand it to you, kiddo,' he said, giving me a cheery slap on the back. 'You certainly got your miracle, didn't you?' And then he gave me a game of Scrabble.

8   Arthur's Farewell

So although the village streets were full of bulldozers and brick-lorries for the next few months, no one was too upset after all. Thanks to Doctor More, only a few houses were built, and they were all arranged in small blocks with names like 'Avalon Court' and 'Camelot Close'.

The pond itself was cleared of any remaining junk, then left in peace for the animals and the Badger Man to enjoy. Not forgetting the Natterjack Toad, of course, who was the real hero of this story in a way.

And Arthur's Oak still stands there, guarding our village like a kindly giant.

But strangely enough, the Knights of the Round Table never met there again. Not as knights, anyway. I suppose the game had run its course, and everyone was ready for something new. I couldn't really blame them. For one thing, Hallowe'en was coming up in the next day or so, and that meant most of my friends were in the mood for ghost stories and monster make-up.

All the same, there was one more event that I ought to tell you about, and it was connected with Hallowe'en too. You see, Jenny's mad aunties were so excited by everything that had happened, that they decided to organise a grand party for all their friends in the village. This took us all by surprise, because hardly anyone had seen inside the round house for years, apart from Jenny and people like the gas man.

Of course, they arrived at the rectory to give their invitations just as Mum was dishing up our supper, but when she saw their faces she couldn't be cross. They fluttered into our dining room like a pair of twittering pigeons, and they spoke in turns as usual.

'We want to celebrate,' said Aunt Ava.

'The trees. And the pond. And the chalice,' said Aunt Lonnie.

'So you will come, won't you?' they finished together.

I was bursting with curiosity. 'What sort of party?' I asked. 'Do we have to wear our best clothes?' My Sunday shirt was really stiff and itchy, and I hated putting it on.

'Fancy Dress, of course,' said Aunt Ava. 'For October the Thirty-First. Nothing else will do.'

'So you will tell everyone, won't you?' added Aunt Lonnie. 'We want it to be a proper village party. Like in the old days.'

'Yes, the old days,' echoed Aunt Ava happily. 'Crowds and crowds of us. All together. A proper village party.'

So that's exactly what happened. About a hundred people turned up, some in Hallowe'en costumes, and the rest in any sort of outfit they could find at such short notice. My father put studs round his oldest dog collar, and went as the Hound of the Baskervilles. Mum went as a Fairy Godmother, and Kit fixed an 'S' to his blue tracksuit, so he could go as Superman.

Most of my gang came as knights, with crumpled shields and woolly helmets covered in tin foil. Lanky's Mum had made him a chain-mail jacket using a collection of old milk bottle tops, and the three Garys came as a three-headed monster which spent the entire evening arguing with itself. And as for me—I was King Arthur. What else could I have been?

Jenny's parents had set up a huge barbecue outside, at the back of the house, but all the rest of the food was spread out on a real round table, just as I had always imagined. I parked myself in the middle of the dining room, on a large round rug, and balanced a plate of charred sausages on my knees while I watched the other guests milling about.

'Great this, isn't it?' said Jenny. 'And we're having a firework display later.' She was dressed as a small witch, in a pointed hat and a long ragged dress. Her dark hair hung in strands round her face, and she had blacked out one of her front teeth.

'Hello, Morgana,' I said, giving her a grin.

'OK,' she laughed. 'But this is definitely the last time. Your Majesty.'

Then Aunt Ava and Aunt Lonnie came scurrying over. They wore their usual loose white clothes, but they had whitened their shrivelled faces with thick layers of powder. They had told everyone they were supposed to be the Brides of Dracula, but as far as I was concerned, they were still the Ladies of the Lake.

'Come on,' they cried. 'Out into the garden. Don't sit here and miss all the fun.'

The next minute, three friendly witches were steering me out of the room and on to the sloping terrace I had only ever seen from the other side of the pond.

Far below me, I could just make out the surface of the water as it glimmered in the moonlight, and I wondered whether the little toad was properly asleep yet. Up here, the air was full of noise and laughter, as people bobbed for windfalls, or lit pumpkin lanterns, but nothing seemed quite real to me.

It was a magical evening, wrapped in smoky smells. People appeared and disappeared amongst the drifting clouds that rose up from the barbecue, and half the time I felt as though I had accidentally rolled into a fantastic dream.

There was Mr Milner, tall and stately in the purple robes of a wizard, talking to a small and sinister executioner. I could tell from the way the dark figure blew his nose that he was really my friend, Doctor More.

Spooks and shadows swirled around me, and a tiny Galahad held up a great silver chalice for everyone to see. The Badger Man rode by on a horse with wheels, chasing a green dragon who just might have been Miss Lane from school. And always, the three witches circled about me, like spirits from another age.

'You must be so proud of your son,' said Aunt Ava to my mother when she came to find me.

'So proud,' repeated Aunt Lonnie. 'So proud.'

'Indeed I am,' said Mum. 'And I always have been. But then, you know, he takes after my side of the family.'

'I do?' I said. This was news to me.

'Yes,' said Mum. 'It was Dad who pointed it out. I'd never noticed before, but you grow more like my own father every day. And he loved animals too, so perhaps that's why you're so interested in toads and trees and things.' And that was when the fireworks began.

Much later, sitting on my own bed at home, I thought over everything that had happened, and I realized that Jenny had been right. I wasn't Arthur any more. I was Adam. Adam Richard Tompkins, just as I had always been.

I looked at Pendragon, curled up at the end of my duvet pretending to be asleep, and I remembered how her arrival had sparked off the whole thing. But although the adventure had ended, I couldn't feel sad.

'Thanks, Arthur,' I whispered through a crack in the curtains. 'It was great while it lasted.'

I wondered where he would go, next time he needed a really good disguise, and if he would choose someone like me again. I hoped he would win that battle too, and that everyone would have as much fun as I had done.

And if you're still thinking I was crazy, I suppose that's up to you. But how else are you going to explain all those coincidences? Morgana and Merlin? Mordred and Galahad? Excalibur and the Ladies of Avalon?

'Good night,' said my father, smiling at me round the bedroom door. 'Sleep well, son. It's a big day tomorrow, don't forget. All Hallows' Day. And thanks to you, I'll be using the proper communion chalice.'

'The Holy Grail,' I thought.

Then I took off my golden crown for the last time, and switched out the light.

ASK ME NO QUESTIONS

Verity just can't help telling fibs, and the bigger the better.

Until the day she eats a sweet given to her by a strange old lady – and then suddenly she can't stop telling the truth! But, surprisingly, the truth gets her into even more trouble than her outrageous fibs ever did. Like when she describes her gran's new hat as an exploding jellyfish.

An entertaining story, full of very funny incidents that show the truth is rarely pure – and never simple.